Gnarlys
of the
NORTH WOODS

Gnarlys of the North Woods

Mary Cuffe Perez

illustrated by Sallie Way

Hobblebush Press
Galway, New York

Cover design and illustrations by Sallie Way

Book design by Colin Rolfe

Distributed by Epigraph Books

Paperback ISBN: 978-1-948796-76-7
eBook ISBN: 978-1-948796-77-4

Library of Congress Control Number: 2019908696

Hobblebush Press
hobblebushpress@gmail.com

Chapter One

The Difference Between Gnomes and Gnarlys

〜◈〜

FIDDLEDUM!

You nearly scared me out of my hide! Do you always go poking about in other creatures' grufs? I see you have never met a Trom before. No, I didn't say Troll. Trolls are ugly. Troms, as you can see, are handsome. Better natured, too. For instance, I'm not going to sic the yellowjackets on you, which the Trolls surely would do.

Come on in, then.

Yes, I live here. Bigger inside than you thought, huh? A lot of creatures, besides me, live inside trees. Birds, raccoons, squirrels, foxes, and one you've probably never heard of. I only know about them because I accidentally spent a winter with one a few years back. Since then, I've been fascinated by these pesky little creatures. I've tracked them throughout their North Woods and taken extensive field notes on their habits; yet, to this day, I can't tell you if they're mice or moles or maybe even a little bit human.

But I do know this: They are the dumbest, smartest, laziest, most adventurous and bothersome creatures in forest or field.

They are Gnarlys.

No, I'm not talking about Gnomes. Now that you're here you might as well stay. I'll tell you a thing or two about Gnarlys and Gnomes.

First, never confuse a Gnome with a Gnarly or a Gnarly with a Gnome. They are not the same, and they do not get along. In fact, they have been feuding for centuries. Everyone's heard of Gnomes, but little is known about Gnarlys. You won't find them in any book. If you *did* happen to see one you would think it was something else—a beetle burrowing underground, a wood frog, wind playing in leaves, or a trick your eyes were playing on you.

Here are the differences between Gnomes and Gnarlys:

Gnomes are old and wise. They have studied how nature works endlessly. It takes two of them to carry the manual, *How Nature Works*. It is their bible and they refer to it constantly. Gnarlys never refer to anything.

Gnomes take care of Nature's business or think they do. They keep things going along as they always have. Gnarlys get in the way of things going along as they always have.

Gnomes are industrious. If you come across a Gnome, you can be sure he will be too busy to talk to you. He may be burying acorns or inspecting leaf buds. He may be counting tadpoles or lecturing caterpillars. He may be collecting acorns or drying wild grapes on a stump in the sun. In the summer, Gnomes are so busy that if you come upon a bumbly blur that is about the size of a chipmunk (minus the tail), it will likely be a Gnome.

Whatever the Gnomes do, Gnarlys undo. Every time something doesn't go just right—a baby bird falls out of its nest, or a squirrel loses the tip of its tail, or a squabble breaks out among the normally agreeable groundhogs—the Gnomes think the Gnarlys had something to do with it.

They are usually right.

Small as they are, Gnarlys have a big talent for making trouble. They make some of their biggest trouble imitating bird and animal sounds. This is their special talent or juju. They imitate sounds so well you cannot tell a Gnarly from a goldfinch, a Gnarly from a leopard frog, a Gnarly from a coyote. This gives them great powers, which they use to make more mischief than the Gnomes have answers for.

Gnarlys say Gnomes have no sense of adventure and Gnomes say Gnarlys are long on adventure but short on sense. This argument has gone on for centuries.

Because of the calamities that Gnarlys cause, Gnomes feel it is their duty to Nature to drive all Gnarlys out of the forest, but hard as they try, the Gnomes have never been able to rid the woods, or Nature, of Gnarlys.

Gnomes claim there are Gnarlys everywhere. Actually, there are very few. To find them, you need to know where to look and how to look. You must also be very lucky. I haven't studied all the Gnarlys in the world, only those who live in North Woods, just over the ridge.

Pull up that tuft of moss. I have a lot to tell you about them.

Field Note

Gnarlys can reproduce the call or song of any bird or animal in North Woods, from crickets to coyotes, and even some that do not live in North Woods any longer but whose call still strikes fear in the hearts of the inhabitants of the forest.

—— Chapter Two ——

The Gnarly Beggin

∿ා⌀

THE Gnarlys of North Woods are Netherby, Nodwart, and Newt. Gnarly names always begin with the letter N. I don't know why.

Hold on. Let me put a log on the fire. There's a chill in the air. By the way, before you put a log on the fire, always check to make sure there are no Gnarlys curled up asleep inside. Sometimes Gnarlys get caught in a snowstorm and can't make it back to their mother tree—or "gruf" in Gnarly terms—so they crawl inside a hole in a log like this one. Nope, no Gnarlys. If there were, I would wake him gently and tell him that he could stay only if he didn't cause any trouble. But that's not likely. Gnarlys make trouble like clouds make rain.

The Gnarlys of North Woods make the biggest downpour of trouble of any creature I know. Even though Gnarlys don't have *How Nature Works* to refer to, they can be very clever and there's always one Gnarly in a group who comes up with big ideas—big ideas that just get bigger and bigger until they break wide open like a thundercloud and the next thing you know there's a Gnarly swept downstream, or a Gnarly dangling from a deer's antler or chased down a mole hole. Most of these big ideas end up with the Gnarlys in big trouble with Gnomes.

Netherby became leader of the North Woods Gnarlys because he is the only one who comes up with big ideas and because neither Newt nor Nodwart have any ambitions for leadership. It is a rare Gnarly who does, and for this reason, both Newt and Nodwart are in awe of Netherby and go along with his ideas even when there is always something better to do.

(Things that are always better to do: Sleep in the sun; eat until you are sleepy enough to sleep in the sun.)

❧

From the height of a human—even from your height—the North Woods Gnarlys look very much alike. But if you were able to get close enough, you would see that each are very different from the others.

Netherby is quite handsome as Gnarlys go. He is just a centimeter or so taller than the other two, which is a lot when you are the size of . . . well, your big toe. His fur is long and sleek and the chestnut hue of a deer in summer, and, like a deer, his fur turns the color of tree bark in winter.

Netherby cares a great deal about his appearance and has been known to stop in the midst of a desperate retreat from rampaging Gnomes to catch his reflection in a pool of water.

Newt is the smallest of the three Gnarlys. He is quite meek and when he becomes nervous, his hands fidget like he is shuffling an imaginary deck of cards. Unlike Netherby's almond

shaped ears, Newt's are small and round, and he does not have Netherby's fine fur. It stays mouse gray year-round and sticks up in tufts. One tuft shoots up between his ears like his brain had a minor explosion. While most Gnarlys of North America have black eyes, Newt's are moss green, like the Gnarlys of Nova Scotia and Newfoundland.

For all he lacks in appearance, Newt makes up for in juju. He has more juju than the other two. He can imitate any animal sound so well it can fool not only the Gnomes but Nature herself.

Last of the North Woods Gnarlys is Nodwart. And Nodwart usually is. Last, I mean. He has a hard time keeping up with the others, being the roundest and not especially interested in keeping up. His fur is even more special than Netherby's fine fur, because it can change with his mood or the time of year—from green and black to gold and brown, and in the winter it turns completely white. This makes Nodwart the best camouflaged of the Gnarlys. A Gnome or a hungry fox could be inches away while Nodwart was fast asleep—which he often is—and pass right by.

Nodwart's sleepy expression goes with his sleepy nature. He is the least likely of the Gnarlys to get big ideas or even a very small one. Still, Nodwart has even more Gnarly luck than the others, which makes up for a lot.

Did I mention that North Woods Gnarlys often wear uniforms? Not all Gnarlys wear uniforms, but the North Woods Gnarlys do. At least, they do when they are on expedition. Netherby, the leader of this particular beggin (that's Gnarly for "group" or "squadron") believes that no serious expedition should be undertaken without the benefit of uniforms.

Where do their uniforms come from? Mostly from the forest floor. They use discarded beetle wings tied together with spider web silk. Of course, the beetle must be dead, and the spider web vacated. The prickly husks of beechnuts serve as their helmets. For the most serious expeditions, they carry lances, which are porcupine quills and highly prized Gnarly possessions.

The uniforms, as you can imagine, are not very comfortable and only Netherby makes a habit of wearing his. Newt and Nodwart are always grumbling about their uniforms, which are either sliding off or tripping them up.

When Gnarlys aren't on expedition, outwitting the Gnomes, or pestering birds, they will probably be fast asleep inside their gruf. You can see it from here, just on the other side of Alder Creek in North Woods. They live in the cavity of a two-hundred-year-old sugar maple they call Sweet Fat Mama, the largest tree in North and South Woods. She is much larger than this old oak I live in. Small as they are, Gnarlys need lots of room.

Sweet Fat Mama is the center of the Gnarly world. She looms large on Highbush Hill overlooking Alder Creek, giving the Gnarlys a good view of the approach of their archenemies, the Gnomes, should the Gnomes dare approach their gruf. Though the entrance at the base of Sweet Fat Mama looks like a welcome, the Gnomes and other intruders know it is a trap. The tree is surrounded by a Gnarly defense system so cleverly concealed that occasionally a careless Gnarly falls victim to his own trap.

Gnarlys come and go from Sweet Fat Mama through a secret network of tunnels and passageways leading into and out of the gruf from several locations. Keeping their gruf secure is essential to Gnarly survival.

As I mentioned before, Netherby is the one who gets big ideas. Newt is the one who worries about the "how" of these big ideas. Nodwart is seldom bothered by either of these concerns.

Field Note

The Gnarlys love Sweet Fat Mama for her shelter and security and for the sugary sap that runs down her trunk when a pileated woodpecker taps on her bark just right. That is the only way Sweet Fat Mama will give sap. As often as they have tapped, knocked, then pummeled Sweet Fat Mama, the Gnarlys have never gotten any sap from her.

—— Chapter Three ——

Netherby's Big Idea

❧

NETHERBY was chewing on a bitter red oak acorn when he got his next big idea.

I forgot to mention another part of Netherby's uniform. It often includes a scarf fashioned out of Spanish moss, which is not a moss at all, but a trailing lichen that hangs from the branches of the black spruce that grow in Blackfoot Bog. Netherby thinks his scarf adds flair. When he gets a big idea, he twirls the scarf around his neck like a cape. Probably he would prefer a cape but wisely decided against it since it would surely trip him up on expeditions.

"Wouldn't it be fine," he said, "to have a forest of beech trees growing around Sweet Fat Mama, so we could eat sweet beech-nuts while we sip sweet sap and have all the husks we need for our helmets without ever leaving North Woods?"

The other two Gnarlys grunted sleepily.

All three were stretched out in the morning sun of a late summer day, just beyond the shade of Sweet Fat Mama. They had been kept awake all night by a barred owl which perched on a high branch of Mama and hooted from moonrise to sunrise to a barred owl in another tree. Netherby, feeling leadership was called for, had signaled the beggin to suit up and prepare for an attack on the bird. But because owls are one of the most feared predators of the forest, the Gnarly attack proceeded no further than the assembling of uniforms.

"Beechnuts are sweeter than hickory nuts and much sweeter than acorns," said Netherby.

Newt yawned. "So, fetch your rucklesack, Netherby, and bring us beechnuts from South Woods." Newt had just dined on the last of the wild blueberries and was enjoying the feel of the sun on his furry belly.

"As usual, you think too small, Newt," replied Netherby impatiently. "Our very own forest of beech trees, growing right here. Picture it!"

If there was work in the picture, the other two Gnarlys wanted no part of it. Besides, the Gnarlys had suspended all expeditions to South Woods since humans had been seen there. They scrunched deeper into the moss and tried their hardest to sleep. But Netherby was on his feet now and leaning over both, throwing his shadow across their squished-up faces.

"*We'll show those Gnomes,*" Netherby added.

Newt and Nodwart unsquished their faces. Their ears pricked up. Gnarlys love to *show those Gnomes* almost better than Gnarlys love wild blueberries. The threat of humans suddenly seemed far away.

"But there isn't a single beech tree in North Woods," Newt replied, giving the idea some consideration.

"Not *now*," replied Netherby. "We have to plant them!" He strode back and forth, feeling very important in his Gnarliness. "Remember, Gnarlys think of things Nature forgot. Not like Gnomes, who always have their big noses tucked inside *How Nature Works* so they can pester Nature about what she already knows and was about to do anyway." He twirled his scarf around his neck. "Gnarlys are Nature's soldiers. Gnomes are nags."

"Hmm . . . That means a lot of beechnuts," said Newt, "inside a lot of prickly beechnut husks. How do we carry them from South Woods to North Woods?"

"Carry?" exclaimed Netherby. "A Gnome would carry them. A Gnarly would get someone else to carry them."

Newt and Nodwart stared blankly at Netherby. "Who?" they asked in unison.

Netherby didn't answer. His eyes darted about like pinballs, and his ears twitched. Nodwart and Newt would have to wait until the idea settled into place and Netherby decided to tell them what it was.

All he said for now was: "We will use our best stealth . . ."

Field Note

⌣

Small as they are, Gnarlys are not very good at stealth. They are clumsy and loud. They fall over things. They complain about what they have fallen over. They make a lot of noise telling one another to stop complaining about whatever it is they have fallen over.

⌣

—— *Chapter Four* ——

Expedition to South Woods

❧

THE Gnarlys stalked through North Woods, ducking under mushroom caps, crawling under fallen leaves, wriggling through forests of ground cedar and club moss, and diving between tree roots when a blue jay swept too close. They scaled a boulder, digging their toes into footholds of crevices and beds of lichen. It was an exhausting climb in full uniform carrying their rucklesacks.

The three sat atop the boulder to get their bearings and have a rest amid a miniature forest of lichen, moss, ferns, and birch seedlings that had sprung up where soil had collected in crevices. Crouched in the shade of a Christmas fern, the Gnarlys scanned the forest for predators or a party of Gnomes before starting down the other side. They had difficulty maneuvering the slope, and Nodwart, being the best climber up but not down, went head over big feet the last few inches, his rucklesack thumping behind him.

They skulked toward South Woods, on the other side of Alder Creek, signaling and making secret calls back and forth. To cross the creek, they balanced along a fallen branch carrying their rucklesacks. This was risky because Gnarlys are not very good swimmers and if a hawk spied them, they would have been easy pickings, especially since Netherby had decided their lances would not be useful for this particular expedition.

By the time they had crossed the creek into South Woods, they were tired and disheveled, their beetle wings dragging behind them. But the woods were full of beech trees mixed with oaks, and Nodwart and Newt went straight to work deftly extracting the tender beechnuts from their prickly husks, then popping them into their mouths.

"Fill your rucklesacks first," demanded Netherby. "Then your stomachs."

Grumbling to each other that Netherby sounded more like a Gnome than a Gnarly, Newt and Nodwart went to work removing the nuts from their husks. Nodwart, whose hands could not fit inside the opening in the husks, stomped on them to crack them open with his large feet.

Finally, their rucklesacks were stuffed with beechnuts, some still in their husks as the Gnarlys were eager to get on with stuffing themselves.

Their stomachs full, all three burrowed under a pile of duff and fell contentedly to sleep.

～❧～

"Adjust your uniforms," Netherby shouted, startling the Gnarlys out of sleep which startled a partridge into flight which startled a deer feeding nearby. Unfortunately, a deer was an essential part of Netherby's plan.

"That's the wrong deer anyway," Netherby grumbled as the deer bounded away. Newt and Nodwart turned to him questioningly. "I'll let you know when it's the right one," was all Netherby said.

Sometime later, Newt and Nodwart were rudely awakened again. Netherby was jabbing them with a twig. "That's the right one," he whispered excitedly. The sleepy Gnarlys gazed upon a buck grazing on acorns. It looked like a mountain range with antlers.

"Okay, beggin, grab your rucklesacks and take your positions!" Netherby demanded.

"Positions?" Nodwart and Newt stared at their leader in confusion.

"Up there!" Netherby hissed, gesturing toward the mountainous deer.

Since the Gnarlys were officially on expedition, they had no choice but to follow Netherby's orders. Terrified and trembling as they were, the Gnarlys tunneled through leaves until they were close to the grazing buck.

Nodwart, whose fur had changed from green and black to brown and gold, went first. Swinging his rucklesack over his back, he dashed from under cover, attached himself to the deer's hind leg and climbed. Nodwart's big feet and hands are good for something besides tripping over. As the best climber, he always goes first.

Once atop the deer, Nodwart dug his fingers and toes into the thick fur between the deer's shoulders and gazed down on the other two struggling up behind him. He hoped there would be no more orders coming his way.

Nodwart, being a little dim, still had no idea what the deer had to do with Netherby's plan. Newt, who climbed up next, seemed to know. He stationed himself on top of the deer's head, between its ears. Netherby followed and crouched behind Newt. When he tapped Newt on the backside, the smallest Gnarly nodded knowingly. The master of calls, he stretched his neck out so far, he was almost inside the deer's ear and let out the howl of a hungry wolf.

Now, there has not been a wolf in North Woods, South Woods, the entire Adirondack region, or the state of New York for more than one hundred years. But the buck didn't know that. Its ears snapped back as if to ask, "Say that again?" Newt let out another howl, with more notes in it this time. The buck got the message. It rocketed into the air, unaware of the three Gnarlys clinging to its fur.

When the buck came down, he dashed east. Then, Newt howled into the right ear, and the deer plunged north across Alder Creek and into North Woods.

The plan was working perfectly.

Through fur and blur, the Gnarlys could see branches parting like water as they soared skyward, then plunged earthward. Then, somewhere between sky and earth, Sweet Fat Mama rose up ahead. In a flash, Newt and Netherby saw the flaw in the plan.

Stopping.

"Bail out!" called Netherby as the deer swept past Sweet Fat Mama.

Netherby and Newt let go of the buck's ears and sailed through space, bounced off an oak, tumbled to earth, and rolled through leaves. They came to rest, finally, beneath a hemlock, just downhill from Sweet Fat Mama. Distantly, they heard the deer crashing through the underbrush as it plunged deeper into the woods, still heading north.

Netherby and Newt examined themselves for damage. Their uniforms and helmets were gone. Their rucklesacks filled with beechnuts were nowhere in sight. And neither was Nodwart. Poor, terrified Nodwart had been unable to untangle his fingers and toes from the deer's fur.

"A little too much wolf!" Netherby snorted to Newt. Then, with a toss of his scarf, all that remained of his uniform, he stomped off toward the gruf. Newt still stared off into the distance that now held the deer and Nodwart. He wondered how far they would go. It might be days, he thought, before Nodwart found his way back to Sweet Fat Mama, if ever. Unlike Gnomes, Gnarlys have a poor sense of direction.

The North Woods Gnomes and Nubbins (Nubbins are apprentice Gnomes) had also undertaken a mission to South Woods on that day. They were busily burying acorns they thought Nature had overlooked when the buck thundered past as if pursued by a pack of wolves, which was just what the buck thought.

Thinking humans had panicked the deer, the Gnomes pre-pared to escape down one of their Just-in-Case holes when one of the Nubbins, jumping up and down excitedly, announced he spied a Gnarly attached to the deer's hide.

"Another Gnarly hunting expedition, I suspect," replied the Oldest Gnome with a twinkle of his blue eye. The Nubbins laughed out loud until the Oldest Gnome gave them a stern look.

Laughter interrupts work, so you will seldom see a Gnome laughing. For that matter, you will seldom see a Gnome. If you do, never, never mention Gnarlys. This will certainly turn them against you.

As I said, their feud has gone on for centuries.

Field Note

While it is difficult to see Gnarlys in the wild, especially if they are camouflaged, like Nodwart, it is possible, if you have exceptional hear-ing, to detect their snoring. The Gnarlys of North Woods, for instance, have distinct snores. Netherby's is a series of snorts and whistles, Newt's snore is like the lilting song of the winter wren, and Nodwart's sounds like the croak of a bullfrog. If you hear all of these sounds mixed up together coming from inside a hollow tree, you may have come upon a Gnarly gruf.

—— *Chapter Five* ——

Nodwart's Journey to Way-Way Yonda

❧

NODWART changed from brown and green to gold and black and back again so many times he finally turned white.

South Woods, North Woods, the sky and forest spun by. Spurred on by Newt's hungry wolf call that still echoed in his memory, the deer plunged through spruce and pines and hemlocks and beech and bracken and thickets and stream, over a stone wall, upland and lowland. It took Nodwart where none of the Gnarlys had ever been. Though he had finally untangled his fingers and toes from the deer's fur, he was now stuck to the deer by a beechnut husk that had been shaken loose from his rucklesack.

He wiggled and kicked and thrashed but could not unstick himself from the husk stuck to the panicked deer.

Finally, the deer dove into a thicket of crabapple so dense that the low thorny branches raked the Gnarly loose from the husk and free of the deer's fur. The deer stopped, looked back, and with a snort as if realizing he, too, had been the victim of a Gnarly trick, trotted off into the deepening darkness of the forest.

Nodwart tumbled through the crabapple thicket, then through bramble and fern until he landed on a mat of sphagnum moss. Soggy, but otherwise unharmed, he sat up and looked around. "Aha," he said, hoping for an idea to come. Unfortunately, Nodwart seldom got ideas, and to make matters worse, like all Gnarlys, he had no sense of what was north, what was south, east, or west.

But Nodwart did know he was in a bad place for a Gnarly to be. Sphagnum moss grows in bogs and bogs are full of Gnarly-hungry predators like turtles and frogs and raccoons, and there was even a plant that Netherby called a pitcher plant that could gulp a Gnarly down whole!

"Not for Nodwart," he said in a quivering voice.

He thought of the welcoming, spreading branches of Sweet Fat Mama on the crest of Highbush Hill. He thought of the other Gnarlys feasting on the last of the blueberries and the dried Mayapples they had raided from one of the Gnomes' storage bins, and he thought of his thistledown nest inside Sweet Fat Mama. He wanted to be home very badly.

The towering ostrich ferns that arched over Nodwart began to rustle and sway. He sniffed the wind and was relieved it carried no news of rain, but it did carry other mysterious and troubling scents that made him even more anxious to get back to the gruf.

He started off, following a deer run through the ferns, happy to find a path going somewhere. He did not realize the deer run led even farther north. Dark shadows crept into the canopy of green, and he could see no end to the forest of ferns.

When a Gnarly is so frightened that there doesn't seem any way out of a predicament, he will curl up into a ball, like a caterpillar or a hedgehog, and hope the danger will pass. Nodwart, who was not especially brave anyway, felt he might be that frightened any minute now. But he also knew that would not get him home. He would have to come up with an idea. Fast.

The Gnarly climbed up on a clump of sword grass. He tried to pry off one of the seed heads but only managed to fumble it away. So, he chewed on the grass blade instead to help him think things over. As he waited for an idea to come, his fur changed back from white to brown and green, a more suitable coloring for his surroundings.

He waited, scrunched his nose up and waited some more. Not a single idea came. The wind swept low through the ferns and grasses, this time telling Nodwart of bullfrogs and bog turtles, raccoons and foxes. A series of croaks gurgled up behind the green curtain of ferns, and he thought he heard the jaw gnashing of that Gnarly-eating plant.

"Not for Nodwart!" he said, his first idea emerging.

The idea was to get higher than the croaking sound. Nodwart dug his fingertips and toes into the bark of a red maple, the tree closest to him, and began to climb. As he scaled bark and branch, he got his second idea: If he climbed high enough, he could see Sweet Fat Mama atop Highbush Hill. Nodwart thought Sweet Fat Mama was the biggest tree in the world and once he climbed high enough to see her, he would know which way to go.

Nodwart had the best feet and hands for climbing but a little too much stomach. He grunted and wheezed his way higher and higher. When he was close to the top of the maple, he leaned back against the trunk. He was very tired and would have fallen asleep right then and there if he wasn't so far, far from home. Once he got his breath, he peeked out through the leaves and gasped.

It was the Way-Way Yonda.

Nodwart, you see, had never seen the Way-Way Yonda. He had never even thought much about it because it was too big for his little brain to hold.

Gnarlys inhabit a very small territory. Surrounding the Gnarly territory is the World at Large, or the Way-Way Yonda, which reaches farther than Gnarlys can imagine. Nodwart, a Gnarly of limited imagination, was seeing that world now.

There was much more of it than he had thought. He gave a little jump of excitement seeing it laid out before him. He would have something to tell Newt and Netherby when he finally found his way home. But home, he realized, must be far away. Sweet Fat Mama was nowhere to be seen in the Way-Way Yonda.

The treetops below told Nodwart that it was becoming the time of year of many colors. There was a hint of yellow among the birches, and here and there the maples struck red, the ash trees, a deep lavender. Soon the deer's fur would change to the color of tree trunks, Netherby would change that color, too, and Nodwart would turn completely white. Only Newt stayed the same color. It was the time of year the Gnomes and all the creatures of the forest began to scurry about in preparation for winter.

He climbed almost to the tip of the branch to get a better look. Beyond, the woods broke open into fields of grasses that swept into stone walls, then more forest of dark green conifers, woven through with ribbons of water, a beaver lodge, and farther still, among trees turning red and gold, flashed a river. But nowhere in the world spread out before him was the familiar sight of Sweet Fat Mama. In fact, nothing looked familiar at all.

He leaned out farther, poked his head through the leaves. Then, farther.

Then, down.

The world began to spin. He was riding one of the maple's bright leaves that had set sail on the wind.

Up, down, then almost over, round and round, this way and that. Nodwart could not tell where in the vast swirling forest below he would land. The wind shifted and chose the creek. It was the main branch of Alder Creek, which ran swiftly toward the river.

Nodwart closed his eyes and clung desperately to the leaf stem. When he opened his eyes, he and the leaf were in the creek. Shoreline rushed by as he rode the current of ripples, bends, and falls. Nodwart was sure any minute he would lose his grip on the leaf and tumble into the cold, roiling waters.

If Nodwart was Netherby he might have leaped for one of the overhanging tree branches as the leaf swept under them, but Nodwart was neither brave nor athletic. He held onto the leaf with all his strength. He might have held on until the creek carried him and the leaf to the river miles away, to be swept into the Way-Way Yonda and eaten by a carp or kingfisher; instead, he ran into the Gnarly luck just in time.

The leaf rushed under a clump of brush in the middle of the creek and continued its journey to the river, leaving Nodwart clinging to the brush by his hands and feet.

Terrified, Nodwart closed his eyes and held on. When he opened them, the brush was moving. He crawled to the top for a better view. The brush was crossing the stream, onto the bank. Then it shook itself, nearly dislodging him.

The gray fox, fleeing the scent of a human, had crossed the stream at just the right moment in the life of the Gnarly.

Nodwart nestled deep into the fox's fur. It reminded him of the thick grasses that grew along Alder Creek on a summer day. He felt warm and secure and without even trying, fell fast asleep. Soon he was snoring his bullfrog snore. The fox, which dined on bullfrogs whenever she had the chance, was puzzled to hear a bullfrog so far from the wetlands. She stopped, looked around, then, unaware of her tiny passenger, hurried on.

Once the fox was sure no humans were pursuing her, she paused to clean her paws and scratch from her thick fur a few ticks along with a lone Gnarly. The fox trotted silently toward her den and Nodwart found himself evicted from his comfortable nest, in the middle of night, in the middle of the forest. Easy prey for an owl.

The moon ducked in and out of clouds. And where was Nodwart now? The fox must have taken him deeper into the Way-Way Yonda. Then, he saw that the fox had taken him just where he wanted to be.

There, in the light of a slip of moon, the outstretched branches of Sweet Fat Mama.

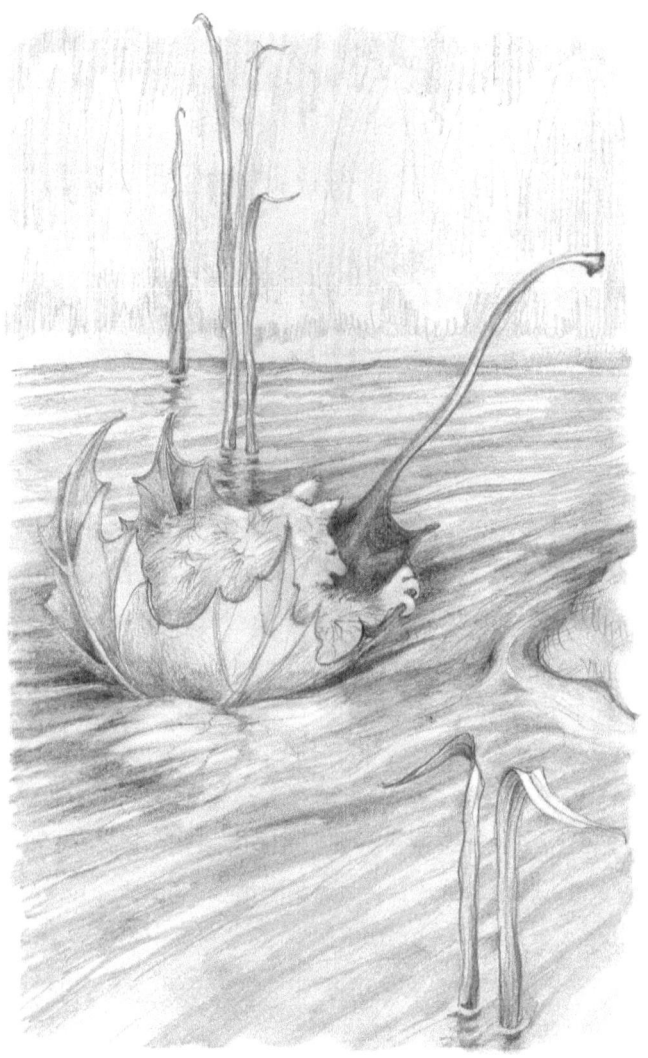

Field Note

*The luck of Gnarlys is legendary. If not for good fortune, Gnarlys would
have gone extinct long ago for they have few practical survival skills.*

─── *Chapter Six* ───

Those Know-It-All Gnomes

❧

NEWT couldn't sleep. He missed Nodwart's bull-frog snore. Netherby did not sleep either, but he would never admit to Newt that he, too, was worried about Nodwart. From time to time, one or the other would get up and peer out the entrance of the gruf into the moonlit forest.

It was in the deepest part of night when Newt caught sight of a form, briefly touched by moonlight, darting toward Sweet Fat Mama. He turned to wake Netherby but Netherby was standing right behind him.

They stood aside as Nodwart wiggled up into the gruf from one of the tunnels.

"Where did the deer take you, Nodwart?" Newt asked.

Nodwart tried to explain the blurry forest, the tree, the world from up high, the leaf, the fall, the creek, the fox. But it took too many words.

"The Way-Way Yonda," he said at last, "and Sweet Fat Mama wasn't there!"

He could not explain any more. He was very tired and though the other two had saved the last of the Mayapples, or a bite of one anyway, Nodwart waved it away and found his thistledown nest, which he had been thinking about since his tumble from the deer. He climbed back into the same deep sleep that the fox had so rudely interrupted.

Nodwart wouldn't hear any more plans from Netherby until three days later when another unusually warm fall day offered the Gnarlys a chance to stretch out in front of Sweet Fat Mama as if the deer incident had never occurred, as if not a predator threatened, as if winter was many months away and there were endless warm, sun-speckled days ahead.

Nodwart and Newt were fast asleep when Netherby returned from another spying expedition on the Gnomes. He was dressed in full uniform. A spray of pod silk was stuck in his scarf from his hiding place, behind a grove of milkweeds. His breath came in short blasts as he paced around the two outstretched Gnarlys, jabbing his lance into the ground with each step. Just a glimpse of Gnomes always put Netherby in a fighting mood.

The particular Gnomes that Netherby had been spying on— the only Gnomes that concern him—are the North Woods Gnomes. Though they are a small troop—three Gnomes and two Nubbins—they are part of a larger Gnome network. If help is needed, they can call upon other parties of Gnomes in neighboring woods by sending a message with a Voped (an orphaned vole carefully trained for this purpose).

This system has enabled Gnomes to flourish worldwide. The Gnarlys, as you might guess, have no such system and cling to survival by their luck and juju.

"Those know-it-all Gnomes!" Netherby punctuated each word with a thrust of his quill lance. "They say it will be an early winter."

Sunlight pouring through Sweet Fat Mama cast leafy shadows across the forest floor and the three Gnarlys. Newt looked up into the leaves overhead. For the first time, he noticed that they were turning colors on the edges. Far off, Canada geese honked their way south.

"Nodwart," he said, sitting up as the thought came to him. "I think winter's coming. *Again.*"

Nodwart shrugged and yawned. He could not imagine any season other than the one that was warming his furry belly at the moment. Even though he had seen the changing colors from high atop the maple, that belonged to the Way-Way Yonda.

Newt turned to Netherby. "Are you sure? Just because the Gnomes say so. Maybe winter won't come this year."

Netherby knew better. Winter came every year. Sometimes it was a winter of deep snow and sometimes it was a winter of bare cold. Sometimes it came before the leaves fell and sometimes it came after. But there was no getting around winter.

"Of course winter is coming, you fruit fly," he snorted. "Have you ever known a winter that just stood back and let it be summer all year? Of course not! Winter's not like that. Winter always comes, but it never lets you know just when. No one knows if it's going to be an early or a late winter. Not even those Gnomes with their pestering of crickets, prying into buds, and popping their eyes over whatever it says in that book of theirs."

Every time Netherby thought about the Gnomes and their manual, *How Nature Works*, it made him angry all over again.

Netherby paced in circles, tossing his scarf and thrusting his lance into the air while the other two Gnarlys fell back asleep in the sun. Nothing infuriated him more than the Gnomes thinking they knew so much. He spied on the Gnomes regularly just to keep up on what they thought they knew.

Netherby was sure he knew as much about how Nature works as the Gnomes, even without a manual. He knew all the signs of winter: The hibernation of the woolly bears, the spiders pulling in their webs, the birds leaving their nests for the Gnarlys to use as observation towers, the hush over forest and field after the last of the geese had flown. Netherby also knew you couldn't say when winter will be or what it will be.

"The Gnomes think they know so much," he grumbled. He pulled milkweed silk out of his scarf. As he let it drift through his fingers on the breeze his eyes began to bounce around in his head. Then his ears flicked backward and forward, and his nose twitched.

If you could climb inside his Gnarly brain you might see a scene like this:

Gnomes filling their dens and emergency burrows (Just-in-Case holes) for winter with nuts and seeds, honey and pollen cakes, dried mushrooms and wild apples. Gnomes battening down the hatches and preparing for a long winter underground. Gnomes settling down on cushions of cotton grass gathered from Blackfoot Bog during the summer, not to doze or dream on, but to plan for the next year.

While it is winter, Gomes will only venture outside occasionally; trekking through snow to make sure winter is going according to plan. But mostly they will keep to their dens. Leaving the woods to Gnarlys.

During a *real* winter, Gnarlys keep to their own gruf, as well, curled up fast asleep most of the time, only venturing out to raid the Gnomes' Just-in-Case holes or a red squirrel's stash of acorns or pine nuts. In a *real* winter, the Gnarlys could not make much use of having the whole woods to themselves.

"All we have to do," said Netherby, his black eyes darting, "is make it *seem* like winter. An early winter, just like the Gnomes said."

"No deer?" asked Nodwart, startled awake.

Netherby was too excited to answer. He paced back and forth. Once in a while he made a little leap in the air. He twirled his lance overhead like a baton. Then he swung around to Nodwart and Newt as if he were about to conduct a symphony.

"They will stay in their den until they *think* spring has come," Netherby announced. "By the time they come out it won't be spring at all. It will be winter. The *real* winter. They won't believe their eyes or ears or even *How Nature Works*!"

"But how," asked Newt, scrunching his entire face into a frown, "do you make winter come early?"

Netherby was done explaining and on to doing. "Come with me!" he ordered.

Even though it seemed too nice a day to do anything other than just what they were doing, Newt and Nodwart yawned, stretched, and got to their feet to follow Netherby. Netherby certainly had a plan, for every other step was a hop—a sure sign of a plan in full bloom.

"Will this require uniforms?" Newt asked droopily.

"Of course. Suit up, men!" called the exuberant Netherby.

Fortunately, the Gnarlys happened to have all the pieces they needed for their uniforms cast about the gruf. This meant they did not have to delay their mission hunting down beetle wings or collecting spider webs to secure the beetle wings or journeying into South Woods to collect beechnut husks. The porcupine quill lances are cherished armaments and stored in secret recesses of the gruf.

As the other two followed Netherby, he revealed only small bits of the plan; not because it was a secret, but because it was still coming together, bit by bit, word by word. He assured the other two that it did not involve large animals, humans, or the least danger. Not so far, anyway.

He knew the beginning and the end of the plan, just not the middle yet. The ending was the best part and he imagined it over and over: The Gnomes' bewilderment when they climbed out of their den after a long Gnarly-made winter expecting it to be spring and finding the real winter instead. Netherby loved this part, especially the look on the Gnomes' faces. He was sure the middle of the plan would fall into place.

∽◉◠

First, the Gnarlys had to track down the Gnomes. When Netherby spied on the Gnomes earlier and overheard their conversation about the early winter, they were huddled around a woolly bear on the downslope to Alder Creek.

The Gnarlys pounced and crept through the woods in their usual pursuit posture, stopping frequently to rest and gaze around themselves. It began to dawn on them what the forest was up to. Summer was packing up, getting ready to leave, tossing leaves, and dropping acorns as it left.

The Gnarlys didn't want summer to leave, but fall gave them beautiful leaves to go dozy watching as they fell. The beech leaves were now turning a rich bronze color, the fiddling of the crickets reached a high, anxious pitch. Flocks of cedar waxwings, preparing for the long flight south, clustered on wild grapevines that twisted through the poplars. The woodpeckers sent volleys of rapping sounds through the woods as they drilled into tree bark in search of insects.

So much activity made Newt and Nodwart sleepy, and they began to stagger toward dozing off until Netherby gave each a jab of his lance. Grunting and grumbling, they resumed their pursuit of the Gnomes. They thrashed through leaves, fell into a vole tunnel, followed it until they surfaced in a thicket of hay-scented fern. Sometimes they scampered through hollow logs or used their lances as catapults. Nodwart tried to hitch a ride on a passing shrew, but the shrew was having none of it.

By the time they got to the spot where Netherby had last seen the Gnomes, the Gnomes were gone. A family of wild turkeys was pecking through the leaf litter in the clearing where the Gnomes had been.

"Oh, well," said Newt.

"Lunchtime!" said Nodwart. "Let's see if we can beat the turkeys to the rest of those partridgeberries."

Netherby swung around to face the other two, hands on his hips. "Beggin!" he shouted. "We are on mission! Track down those Gnomes!"

The Gnarlys continued their mission by following what they thought were Gnome tracks but really belonged to a squirrel.

Field Note

⁓

A Voped is a woodland vole that, as a voling, was driven from its nest by its more robust siblings. Gnomes rescue the runt voles and train them as messengers to Gnomes in other territories. Since voles tunnel underground and through snow, they also create many of the pathways that Gnarlys travel through.

⁓

Chapter Seven

The Incident of the False Winter

∿☙∾

THE Gnarlys followed the scurrying of the squirrel for a while, then the trail of pine cone scales left by a chipmunk, then the scratches of wild turkey kicking up leaves from the forest floor, then their own imaginations. This all led them to the tracks of Gnomes. It was just by chance, of course, but you couldn't tell a Gnarly that.

The Gnomes had followed the creek downstream and were now congregated near its banks, on a little dome of bright green apple moss. *How Nature Works* lay open before them. The three Gnomes were gathered over it, their heads close together, forming a peak of red caps. Their conversation sounded serious, as are all things with Gnomes. The Nubbins were standing behind the three trying to look serious, too.

"They are probably discussing the length of a shadow," said Netherby.

The Nubbins were supposed to be paying attention, but the Gnarlys suspected they weren't. One of them yawned, and the other one made a face. Then, they started punching one another behind the Gnomes' backs while the Gnomes droned on over *How Nature Works*. Nodwart couldn't help chuckling, which drew a sharp jab from Netherby. The Gnomes were so absorbed in what they were saying and the Nubbins so absorbed in being bored, they did not suspect there were Gnarlys about.

"Perfect," said Netherby.

"Perfect," repeated Newt. He adjusted his helmet, which never fit quite right because of the tuft of fur that shot up between his ears. "Now what?"

"Now, we make it sound like winter coming."

As I said before, Gnarlys have an uncanny talent for imitating sounds. It is their special juju. It is an awesome gift and has created flocks of trouble for the creatures of the forest, and especially for the Gnomes. I must say, it has created trouble for me a few times, too. This trouble often blows back on the Gnarlys, but the Gnarlys so love making their juju, they seldom think of the consequences.

Gnarlys can imitate sounds better than the brown thrasher. They can make the sound of a wood thrush so true it almost entices the evening to fall, the bark of the Canada geese so rollicking, the season almost turns. They can send rabbits and squirrels diving into burrows with the ululating of the coyote. They can imitate the huff of a frightened deer, the yip of a fox, the gobble of a wild turkey, the wing thunder of a flushed partridge.

And they can make more than bird and animal sounds; they can create the grumble of storms coming, the conversation of trees, even the whisper of a snowflake falling on a dry leaf. Some, but only the very most gifted, can make the peculiar language of humans. A few can make sounds that no one has ever heard before and wish they would never hear again.

Of the three Gnarlys of North Woods, Newt is the best imitator of sounds. In fact, though none of the Gnarlys realize this, Newt probably has the most juju of any Gnarly, and much more than even he suspects.

So, when it comes time to create a particular sound, it is always Newt whom Netherby turns to first. Netherby and Nodwart fill in here and there, but it is Newt who produces the truest sound. So you see, Newt, who is usually so full of questions, did not have to ask how to make the sound of winter coming.

The Gnarlys took their positions just upstream of the Gnomes, hidden behind a hobblebush. Then, after whispering a few practice hisses, whizzes, whooshes, and ooms, Newt let out the sound of winter coming. It was a wind sound of course, but there was more, too. It was the sound of cold. It makes me shiver to think of it.

It made the Gnomes shiver, too, as it whistled past them. They looked up from their reading to listen carefully. When Newt added the wild geese-going call, both Gnomes and Gnarlys looked skyward.

Next, Newt chirped the let's-go-south call of the wood thrush. The wood thrush is the signal bird of northern forests, the first to sense the approach of storm or danger and the first to know when it is time to fly south ahead of winter.

When Newt made the migration call, the birds that had been enjoying the warmth of the day and savoring insects and elderberries became alarmed. They searched out family members. *Is it time?* the sparrows and swallows and finches chipped, fluttering around in confusion.

The disturbance among the birds added to the sense of urgency among the Gnomes. "Sounds like a Nor'easter coming," the Wisest Gnome said. They looked at one another with thunderously serious expressions. Their predictions were right! Early winter was on its way. They had heard it in the insect chatter; they had seen it in the length of the shadows; they had felt it in the air.

"But there's not a cloud in the sky," said the Oldest Gnome. At that instant, as if it was part of the Gnarlys' plan, a fat gray cloud appeared and squatted between the sun and the patch of woods containing the Gnomes. This was enough to convince the Gnomes that winter was just over the hill. They made off for their nearest Just-in-Case burrow to wait out the storm.

As the Gnomes scurried off, the Gnarlys followed at a safe distance issuing winter coming noises until the Gnomes reached the safety of their burrow.

"The best is yet to come," said Netherby triumphantly, as the last round Gnome form bumbled down the burrow.

The plan seemed to gain force by the minute, like an approaching storm. Netherby crept up to the burrow very carefully. He knew the Gnomes would be peering up out of the hole, searching the sky for signs of the on-coming Nor'easter. The other two Gnarlys crawled up beside Netherby. They resisted the temptation to peek down into the burrow and have a good laugh right into the round, puzzled Gnome faces.

"You stay here and make wind sounds," Netherby whispered to Newt. "Nodwart, hold this fern right there. No. Like this. That's it. That blocks the sun from coming into the hole. Now the Gnomes will think the sun has gone under. *Mys-teri-ous-ly,*" he added with a sly wink.

Then Netherby dashed off, leaving the other two to wonder, as they watched the glint of his beetle wing uniform disappear into tree shadow, what additional feature of winter he had tucked in his head.

Newt kept his wind sounds going and Nodwart held the fern just as Netherby had instructed until the two Gnarlys began to wonder if they had missed something important in the plan. But just at the point when Newt's wind sounds were beginning to flutter, Netherby returned, or what the Gnarlys thought was Netherby.

A white ball of fluff, flying out in all directions, was coming over the rise, propelled by two running feet.

The white fluffy ball was milkweed silk—tiny parachutes ready to carry milkweed seeds to distant lands—with Netherby inside. He had carried a milkweed pod all the way from the edge of South Woods, fending off a garter snake and a curious chipmunk.

At Alder Creek, he broke open the pod and floated across the creek inside one half of the pod, on top of the fluff. On the other side, he gathered up the fluff from the pod and continued his journey, somehow, through all this, keeping his prize mostly intact.

Downwind of the burrow entrance, Netherby unraveled the ball of milkweed silk, pulling some from under his uniform and helmet, some from between his toes and inside his ears.

"Now," he said, rubbing his hands together, "this part takes finesse. Stand back!" Fascinated, Nodwart and Newt watched as Netherby delicately plucked strands of milkweed fibers free and let the wind gently float them over the Gnomes' burrow.

Deep inside their burrow, the Gnomes gasped in astonishment.

"Snow this early? It has never snowed this early . . . as I recall," said the Oldest Gnome, scratching the shock of white hair that sprung free when he removed his cap. But there was no way to know for sure. It was too dark to read *How Nature Works*. This Just-in-Case burrow was not supplied with flints, reed wicks, or bees wax bowls.

"What do we do now?" asked a small voice from a dark corner. It was one of the Nubbins who could barely contain his desire for a little excitement.

"We sit it out," came a surly Gnome voice. It was the Wisest Gnome speaking. "It cannot last long. It's an early storm, that's all. Snows of early storms never last. Soon as it passes, we will continue business as usual. Listen, the winds have died down."

"This is very peculiar," said the Foolish Gnome, his eyes shifting back and forth in his head. Though he was known as the Foolish Gnome, he was the first to suspect a Gnarly plan behind the early winter.

Don't be fooled by his title. The Foolish Gnome was once known as the Tracker Gnome, and how he came to be called the Foolish Gnome instead has everything to do with a Gnarly incident. I'll bet you guessed that already.

By the way, are you warm enough? Here, move a little closer to the fire. I fear it will be an early winter for us this year, and Gnarlys will have nothing to do with it. Now, where was I? Oh yes, the incident with the Tracker Gnome, a.k.a. Foolish Gnome.

~❧~

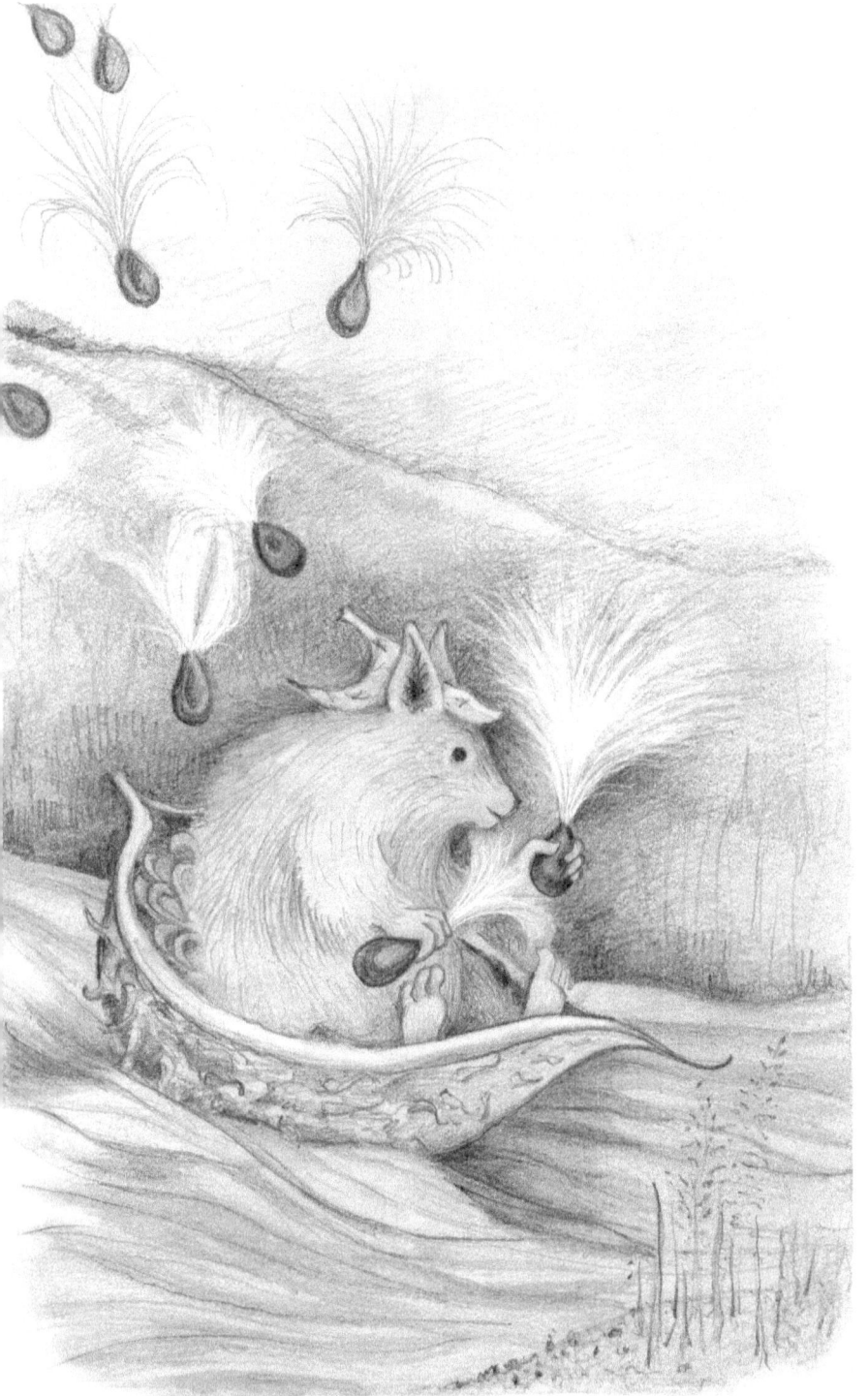

Late one summer afternoon, the Tracker Gnome was hot on the trail of Netherby, who had just raided the Gnome den. *Foolish Gnarly*, the Tracker Gnome thought to himself, *leaving a convenient trail of pollen cake crumbs.* To the delight of the Tracker, the trail led straight down what looked to be a vole's tunnel, only about as wide as the tip of your thumb. The Gnome set off a thunderbomb at one end of the tunnel and waited with his whittlestick at the other.

What flew out of the tunnel wasn't a Gnarly, though. Netherby, who was hidden behind a stone, had trailed the pollen crumbs to the entrance of the hole which led, unfortunately for the Tracker Gnome, to a nest of ground bees. Believe me, you don't want to get on the wrong side of a ground bee. Actually, with ground bees, the wrong side is the only side there is.

These ground bees were so angry about being smoked out of their nest, they chased the Tracker Gnome all the way back to the den where the other Gnomes were just settling down for a peaceful snooze after a long, hard day waking the monarch butterflies from their cocoons. The Tracker Gnome barreled into the den with the ground bees close enough to be a Gnome tail (if Gnomes had tails), having the best fun ground bees can have until they discovered more Gnomes, and suddenly they're having even more fun.

The Gnomes ran hootin' and hollerin' around the den and out the den and into the forest where they dove down one of their Just-in-Case burrows, kicking up dirt behind them to fill the entrance just before the ground bees *zizzed* in.

They stayed that way, in the dark, for two days. That's how long a ground bee's bad temper lasts. After two days, the ground bees went back to their business; the Gnomes, still sore in body and ego, returned to theirs, and the Tracker Gnome was thereafter known as the Foolish Gnome.

You can tell from this story two things: Gnomes don't forgive mistakes—not without a lot of work to undo the mistake—and the Foolish Gnome had a big bone to pick with the Gnarlys.

Getting back to the early winter, the Foolish Gnome's eyes squeezed down to his nose as he thought about the ground bee incident, the strangeness of the early winter and how it all seemed so Gnarly-like. "This is very peculiar," he repeated, trying to sound like the Tracker Gnome rather than the Foolish Gnome. "There was no sign of snow an hour ago."

The Gnomes agreed, but Nature, despite the Gnomes' best efforts, was unpredictable.

Above, Netherby was releasing more and more milkweed silk and urging the other two Gnarlys to resume their wind noises. Soon, a fluffy white layer covered the entrance to the Gnomes' burrow.

"I'll bet it's dark in there," giggled Newt. "They must think they are really snowed in."

"Yes," whispered Netherby. "Let's keep them that way for a while."

He scampered off without further instructions. The other two Gnarlys danced after him, delighted with the success of their plan. With the Gnomes tucked away, there was some mischief to be made in North Woods and some booty to raid from the Gnomes' den.

Field Note

⚊

Gnarlys usually collect their lances from cast-off porcupine quills. Extracting a quill attached to a porcupine requires great delicacy and a very daring Gnarly. Gnomes, on the other hand, carry thunderbombs (puffball mushrooms full of spores that, when released, can momentarily blind or choke the enemy) and whittlesticks, which are the dried shafts of cattails, whittled to a fine point with flakes of flint.

⚊

Chapter Eight

Newt's Juju and the Wood Thrush

⌒৩৲⌒

HEAR that? That's a wood thrush. It's late in the year for a wood thrush to sing or to still be north. A last gift of fall. Listen. Doesn't it make you think of crystal tinkling on air? It is the most beautiful song on earth. You wouldn't think anything could come close to creating the wood thrush song. But the Gnarlys can. At least, Gnarlys with as much juju as Newt has. So, you can understand why the wood thrush, of all the birds, has the biggest grudge against the Gnarlys.

There are plenty of reasons for birds to put Gnarlys Number One on their Most Wanted list. Gnarlys love to torment birds— by switching eggs from nest to nest or setting off a panic with the shriek of a sharp-shinned hawk or the spooky trill of a screech owl. But stealing the wood thrushes' song is, at least to the wood thrush, the biggest crime of all.

Mind that spider web. She's just rewoven it after a nasty bout with a wasp. She won't take kindly to doing it over again. Just move a little this way. That's fine.

As I was saying . . . what was I saying? Oh, yes. Thank you. The biggest grudge the wood thrush has against the Gnarlys is the theft of their song. It's like if . . . let me think. Okay. You're human, right? Say you painted a picture or wrote a song or a poem and then someone came along and copied it exactly and said it was theirs . . . well, that's how the wood thrush feels. It took millions of years for that song to become what it is today, and here a Gnarly snatches it away just for the fun of making mischief. I have to say—it's good! But if a wood thrush asks me, I say right away that I could tell it was a Gnarly imitation and not a real wood thrush song.

Between you and me, Newt's version of a wood thrush song is right on. It is so good I stop what I am doing just to listen. Even other birds see a wood thrush in the song. It has created a lot of frustration among female birds looking for a suitable mate. They are so taken by the song, they follow it right to the furry little pretender who is forced to dive down an escape hole.

Also, the wood thrush is the signal bird. It's a very important job in the bird world. If Newt makes the going-south call for the sheer delight of it, as Newt is likely to do, the birds start spreading the word that it's time to migrate, even if it's mid-summer. Pretty soon, the birds stop believing the wood thrush's going-south call. That puts the thrush out of a job, so to speak.

What do the Gnarlys think about all this? Netherby and Nodwart don't think much about it. The havoc they raise in the world of birds is great fun for them, and occasionally, a way to get out of a jam. But Newt is different. Oh, yes, he has every bit a Gnarly's flair for fun and mischief, but he has another side, too; a side he does not like to reveal to the other two.

You see, Newt is in awe of birds. Their songs bring him to rapture. Often in the early summer, when the other two Gnarlys are dozing in the sun or occupied assembling catapults or traps or spying on the Gnomes, Newt slips away. He finds a suitable jack-in-the-pulpit and settles himself deep inside. He will stay there until nightfall listening to the warblers and sparrows and thrushes. Each trill and warble and coo is stored like a precious keepsake within his memory.

Of all the birds, the wood thrush is Newt's favorite. He has worked long and hard perfecting the bird's heavenly song. He doesn't mean to trick the bird, even if that is the end result. He sings because he loves the wood thrush.

Once I witnessed Newt and a wood thrush locked in a beautiful asking and answering song on the brink of evening. As sunlight descended, the thrush dropped closer to the call that came from deep inside a jack-in-the-pulpit. The bird perched on the very rim of the pulpit to deliver her answer. Newt, so overcome by the song and the nearness of the bird, slipped out of his hiding place inside the pulpit and spilled onto the ground.

"A Gnarly!" shrieked the thrush, startling Newt out of his revelry. "A nasty little Gnarly!"

Newt peered bleary-eyed up at the bird. "Can't we sing a little longer?" he pleaded. "Just a little longer. No tricks, no tricks, I promise."

"No tricks?!" The wood thrush squawked like a raven. "A Gnarly is nothing but tricks!" The bird that had been drawn so close to Newt, now swooped down on him, forcing the Gnarly to scurry back up the stalk of the plant and dive inside for safety. The thrush's warning call, which said in harsh chip, chip, chips: *Don't trust your ears, there are Gnarlys about!* stalked off on the air.

Sometimes, love isn't easy.

Field Note

⁓

The jack-in-the-pulpit is one of the most accommodating plants in the forest. Besides being a convenient shelter for Gnarlys, it offers up red berries on its spadix in the fall, like candy on a stick, for many forest animals.

⁓

Chapter Nine

Hi-Ho a Merry-O, the Gnomes Down a Hole

✦

CRUMBS of pollen cakes, bits of chewed up honey-comb, scattered pieces of dried mushroom caps, half-eaten pine nuts, and tipped over honey pots littered the floor of the Gnomes' den. The Gnarlys, delirious with joy and too much honey, danced amid the rubble, congratulating themselves on their best expedition of the season.

"The Gnomes down a hole, the Gnomes down a hole, hi-ho a merry-o, the Gnomes down a hole," they sang, then howled with laughter, somersaulted over one another and rolled across the floor through the booty of spilled honey and other delights.

The resident Voped did not seem alarmed that there were Gnarlys in the den, rather than Gnomes. In fact, the Voped watched the Gnarlys cavort with merriment in her eyes, though you couldn't tell as a Voped's eyes are very small. She had no special fondness for Gnomes. Except to give her orders, the Gnomes paid little attention to the Voped, especially during the last few weeks when they were preoccupied with getting in their winter stores. The Voped had been fed a steady diet of acorn mush, which she found distasteful. But the Gnarlys were generous souls and shared the bounty of raided Gnome supplies which were usually kept well out of her reach.

Eventually, Nodwart and Newt wore themselves out and collapsed between a hi and a ho in the middle of the den. Netherby, who was far from sleepy, gazed upon the other two and shook his head. Crumbs covered them head to toe, sticking to their honey-coated fur. Nodwart had fallen atop the smaller Newt, his large feet sticking straight up in the air. Not a shred of their uniforms remained.

As Newt's lyrical snore punctuated the flat notes of Nodwart's snore, Netherby settled back to consider how the Gnarlys could make the most of this rare and wonderful Gnomelessness. His eyes wandered about the den. Despite the raid and all the Gnarlys' attempts to ravage the den's orderliness, there was still a Gnomeness about it, which was as infuriating as it was impressive.

Netherby strode across the den and kicked up the Gnomes' neatly arranged bedding of ground cedar, then plopped down on it to think about everything that irritated him about the Gnomes. The Voped watched him lazily, then closed her eyes and joined the other two Gnarlys in sleep, leaving Netherby to his brooding.

It was growing dark, but Netherby did not know how to light the reed on the beeswax bowl in the corner of the Gnomes' den, so he sat with his hands across his stomach in the attitude of a Gnome and thought about all the Gnome injustices against Gnarlys. There was a lot to think about.

It is the Gnome mission, as part of their duty to serve Nature, to rid the world of Gnarlys. If a Gnome spies a Gnarly, he will drop what he is doing, grab his whittlestick and chase the Gnarly for as far as his breath will take him.

Then, there is that word, "nuisance," the Gnomes so frequently spit at the Gnarlys; as if a word that would better describe a mosquito could define a Gnarly.

But the very worst of it, Netherby thought, rising and pacing around the other two loudly snoring Gnarlys, was the crude demolition of the Gnarly works of genius. Netherby's works of genius.

Like the dam on Alder Creek, for one.

It was two summers ago, the hottest summer in many years. Gnomes and Gnarlys and creatures of the forest gasped through the heat. The birds fanned their young constantly with their wings, the squirrels panted prone on tree limbs, the frogs and turtles and salamanders retreated deep inside the earth much as the Gnarlys did, down one of the tunnels leading into and out of Sweet Fat Mama.

It was so hot that the Gnomes, in order to carry on their Gnome business, did something they almost never do—peeled off the red caps and green jackets they were so proud of.

While Newt and Nodwart were content to sleep away the hot spell, Netherby was not. Who else would have come up with the idea to dam the creek to make a nice little swimming hole for Gnarlys? This plan called forth Netherby's greatest engineering achievement, involving the services of an unsuspecting box turtle to carry the first anchoring branch across the creek while Netherby worked tirelessly to keep the other two Gnarlys on task filling in the rest of the dam. Netherby considered it his masterwork.

Gnarlys are not very good swimmers but they do enjoy a nice still pool where they can back float or sail on oak galls. And for a day and a half that's just what they had.

That's all the time it took for the Gnomes to get wind of the situation; or rather, the trickle of the situation, which was all that was left of Alder Creek for the animals, amphibians, birds and Gnomes downstream.

"The injustice!" Netherby snorted. The incident came back to him in every detail: The startling sight of near-naked Gnomes (Gnome bodies are furless and white as a frog's belly) storming upstream with raised whittlesticks; the capsizing of Gnarlys from their vessels and the destruction of the dam it had taken days to build. "This is *not* how Nature works," the Oldest Gnome chanted, as he alternately plunged his whittlestick into the remains of the dam and waved it in the direction of the fleeing Gnarlys.

Netherby's chest began to heave. There were other injustices, other works of genius plundered by Gnomes, such as Netherby's On the Wing scheme, to train a fledgling bird (young birds are notoriously gullible) to fly Gnarlys on expeditions and spying missions. Netherby envisioned himself as pilot, secure between the bird's wings, the wind fluttering his scarf as he flew over North Woods, buzzing the Gnomes. The Gnomes got wind of that plan, too, and alerted the parent birds, who put a sharp end to Netherby's fantasy.

Of course, Netherby recalled with a gleeful glint in his eye, there were times when the Gnomes' interference in a Gnarly plan backfired on them.

Just last spring, for instance. It is a spring ritual for Gnarlys to create pandemonium in the woods by terrifying birds with hawk calls. Sparrows, wrens, and catbirds flee in terror, leaving their nests unprotected just long enough for the Gnarlys to switch eggs from nest to nest, a favorite Gnarly tradition.

The Gnomes, of course, feel they have to interfere with this ritual by putting things right.

But Gnomes are not good climbers. They had a terrible time hauling their considerable middle parts up over branches, especially with an egg clutched under one arm, then teetering out to the end of branches to return the proper egg to the proper nest.

It was the Foolish Gnome (once known as the Tracker Gnome) who was caught with his hands on a catbird's precious egg when the bird returned to its nest. An ugly scene followed in which the Foolish Gnome was held hostage by the catbird for several days. It is not one of the oft-told tales in Gnome lore and is certainly not to be found anywhere in *How Nature Works*.

The incident so infuriated the Gnomes that they hunted the Gnarlys relentlessly for three days. But the Gnarlys were tucked safely inside Sweet Fat Mama, laughing so long and hard their laughter echoed inside the great tree and bounced out a woodpecker's hole and into the forest.

Thinking about the Gnomes with their red faces and *wuffaloofs* puffing out of them improved Netherby's mood a little. Next to confusing birds, getting the best of Gnomes is the chief joy of Gnarlys. Confounding Gnomes, Netherby mused, was nothing next to confounding humans, but only crows had mastered that fete. It would be a bold Gnarly to try.

This line of thinking led Netherby down another path—a dangerous path—the path that had been widened by humans into a trail that ran along the far side of the stone wall separating South Woods from the edge of the Way-Way Yonda.

For many years, the human trail led across Alder Creek, along the edge of South Woods, around Blackfoot Bog and into the Way-Way Yonda. But the humans usually stayed on the trail, on the other side of the stone wall, making more noise than trouble.

In Netherby's sightings of humans on the trail, he had made a few observations: They have no season. They are active in the summer as well as in the dead of winter. They step on everything and never look where they are going. They usually come in pairs and they talk and talk and talk. They almost always leave a few useful items behind.

In recent months, he had noticed something else: Humans had removed stones from the stone wall and extended their trail far into South Woods, reaching very close to North Woods.

Human invasion is a threat to Gnomes and Gnarlys alike. If the Gnarlys could chase the humans back onto the trail on the other side of the wall, North Woods and South Woods would be safe again. Even better: The Gnomes would be forced to recognize the superiority of Netherby . . . er, the Gnarlys. They might even devote an entire chapter to Netherby . . . er, the Gnarlys—in *How Nature Works*.

Netherby was enjoying the vision of Gnomes looking humble, of Gnomes removing their red caps in Netherby's presence, of Gnomes bowing before him, while Newt and Nodwart snored loudly around him, tossing in their sleep from the discomfort of too much honey mixed with too much of everything else. At one point, Nodwart sat straight up, said "aha," and fell back to sleep. But Netherby hardly noticed. He was following his plan to the very edge of the Way-Way Yonda.

~◎~

The Way-Way Yonda?

It's not far at all from here. In fact, it's where you come from. It probably doesn't seem that special to you, but to the Gnarlys, it's another universe. The Gnarlys had heard many stories about the Way-Way Yonda, but like the Gnomes, they did not venture there. Even Nodwart, who had seen it from the top of the red maple when he was lost, could not think about it very long without feeling lost again. Gnarlys might talk about traveling to other lands, but they would never choose to leave North Woods, except for occasional expeditions to South Woods.

I've already told you how Gnomes and Gnarlys are different. Well, they have certain traits in common, as well. These are:

Gnomes and Gnarlys both fear humans and crows about equally.

Gnomes and Gnarlys have very limited territories. They do not know much about the Way-Way Yonda.

Gnomes and Gnarlys worship trees.

Remember—they do not think they are alike at all, so never bring it up, if you should ever happen to run across one or the other.

Another thing, if you should run across a Gnarly or a Gnome, do not assume that he or she sees the world the way you do. The Gnarlys' world is very different from the Way-Way

Yonda. A walk across your backyard would be a three-day journey for a Gnarly, fraught with wildlife encounters. A stream you may leap across is a river to a Gnarly. A stone you might rest upon is a mountain to climb. A spider web you would brush aside could be a deadly trap for a Gnarly. The puffball you stamp upon for the fun of watching the spores fly creates a dust storm in the Gnarly world.

The world you hardly see is the Gnarly world.

So, you can understand how the idea that was now becoming a plan in Netherby's mind was his most ambitious ever. It would take the Gnarlys not just into South Woods, but to the very edge of the Way-Way Yonda. It would pit the Gnarly juju against the most powerful force in Nature.

And it would sure show those Gnomes.

Field Note

Of all the tools in Nature that Gnarlys use, oak galls are among their favorites. These are large (one- to two-inches in diameter), rounded growths on oak trees containing a single wasp larva in the center. After the wasp emerges, the gall hollows out and falls to the ground. It makes a perfect Gnarly flotation device or temporary shelter.

Chapter Ten

Do Humans Have Feathers?

~∾~

"**T**IME to check up on those humans," Netherby announced the next morning, mimicking the Gnomes, who were always checking up on sparrow eggs, or the length of the day, or the opening of a leaf bud, or what the Gnarlys were up to. The other two Gnarlys had just awakened. They had returned to Sweet Fat Mama late in the night and were not eager for another Netherby plan.

Nodwart climbed off Newt whose body had gone numb under Nodwart's weight. After they untangled from each other they began picking crumbs from their coats, munching on some, tossing others away. Finally, Netherby's words hit bottom. Nodwart gave a little jump and stared at Netherby in alarm.

"Humans? Humans step on Nodwart," he said with a resolute shake of his head.

"We will observe," said Netherby slyly. "From a safe distance. And maybe warble a note or two."

The other two weren't convinced. Newt scratched the tuft of fur between his ears and Nodwart stared into space, his features compressed into a frown.

"Just for fun," Netherby said with a little hop. "What could be more fun that confounding humans with a call or two?"

There was a flicker of interest in Newt's eyes, but Nodwart's expression was still locked in resistance.

"And humans always leave something useful," Netherby added, looking at Nodwart. "Maybe they'll drop more gooble."

"Gooble!" Nodwart cried. Pure joy spread across his face. Gooble—chewing gum as you know it—is Nodwart's favorite thing. As far as Gnarlys are concerned, the only benefit of having humans in the world is that they leave useful items along the trail, including wads of gooble. Gnarlys have lots of uses for gooble.

"Do we need uniforms?" Newt asked with a sigh.

"Not for this expedition. The Gnomes are down a hole, and we don't have to worry about them huffing and puffing after us with thunderbombs and whittlesticks. Just our rucklesacks and lances, in case we encounter predators."

The Gnarlys broke into dance, which they sometimes do before going out on a major expedition.

The Gnarly dance is a peculiar thing. It involves a great deal of hopping about, tumbling, shaking arms and legs in the air, and finally falling to the ground. Sometimes the dance goes on so long the Gnarlys (or at least Newt and Nodwart) forget what the mission is and fall asleep instead.

Netherby was not about to let that happen this time. He cut the dancing ritual short and, with a toss of his scarf, bounded out of the gruf. He was already halfway down Highbush Hill before the other two caught up.

Together, the beggin scurried off through North Woods, headed for South Woods and the edge of the Way-Way Yonda. They felt very free-spirited and chattered loudly. They did not bother to duck under anything, crawl, scamper, or scurry. The Gnomes, after all, were down a hole.

"Don't forget predators," Netherby shouted over his shoulder, trying to instill at least a little caution in the carefree Gnarlys as they charged through the moss and thrashed fallen leaves with their lances just to make a noise. Netherby's warning blew over them like a dandelion seed on the wind. They did not give a thought to predators or caution. They were thinking how clever they were to fool the Gnomes with the early winter.

Only when they came to the stone wall dividing South Woods from the Way-Way Yonda did their noise-making sputter down to silence. The possibility of humans turned the Gnarlys serious. They crouched in the grass and waited. For a long time, no one made a sound.

"Do they have feathers?" asked Newt finally, shuffling his fingers nervously. He had never seen a human.

Netherby thought hard. "I have never seen one in feathers," he said, "but I wouldn't be surprised to see a human in feathers. They wear many different disguises."

"How Nodwart know?"

"You'll know," replied Netherby. "Nothing else looks like them."

This explanation did not satisfy Newt or Nodwart.

"Do they make a call?" asked Newt.

"Not exactly."

"How will we know when they're coming?" asked Newt in alarm.

"You'll know!" said Netherby, becoming impatient with all the questions.

The Gnarlys sat in silence for a while. Then, "Now what?" pouted Newt. He and Nodwart were beginning to lose interest in the expedition.

"We sit tight and wait," replied Netherby, parting the grasses and scanning the trail.

"Wait" to a Gnarly means "sleep." Newt and Nodwart were asleep before Netherby could turn back around. Netherby was too excited to sleep. His plan was zinging back and forth in his head and he could hardly wait for humans to come along to try it out on.

Although Netherby had a great deal to say about humans, he did not know as much about them as he led the other Gnarlys to believe. He would tell them story after story while stalking earthworms or startling birds, that made the other Gnarlys believe that long before Netherby came to North Woods he had dealings with humans and had learned their ways.

This gave Netherby even higher ranking in the eyes of Nodwart and Newt and was one of the reasons he was their leader. As I have mentioned before, he was also their leader because he was capable of ideas and because neither of the other two Gnarlys had any interest in leadership.

Humans were the reason Netherby lived in North Woods instead of where he was born, in Woods of the White Pine, a few miles from here. Even though humans played a large role in Netherby's early life, all he remembered about them was that they were enormous and terrifying.

Oh, I know, you don't think of yourself as enormous or terrifying, but you have to remember to look at things from the Gnarly point of view, where almost everything in the world is big and scary.

To Gnarlys and Gnomes, humans come from the Way-Way Yonda and are as mysterious as its reaches. To know humans is beyond the knowledge of Gnarlys and Gnomes and anything contained in *How Nature Works*.

It was late afternoon when the earth began to tremble and hum, crash, and rumble. The Gnarlys were shaken from their slumber, hearts pounding.

Something big was coming.

You must be tired. I've told you a lot for one day. If you find your way back to this old oak again, I'll tell you about the Gnarlys' encounter with humans. Oh, yes, and the Gnomes, too. Can't forget the Gnomes down a hole, can we?

Field Note

~

Gnarlys' purpose in Nature is not understood. In fact, even the Gnomes'
comprehensive manual, How Nature Works, *makes scant mention of*
Gnarlys. They are described merely as "... nasty little hairballs that are
a scourge to Nature and a constant threat to her orderly workings. They
must be driven out wherever they infest." It's easy to see that a Gnome
wrote How Nature Works.

~

—— Chapter Eleven ——

Newt's Big Moment

⁓∽

THANKS for knocking this time.

No, no yellowjackets. Come on in. It's getting cold out there. I'll be hibernating soon, once my firewood runs out and the snows cover the entrance to the oak. You won't find me at all then. So, I'd better get this story told. Let's see. The humans were approaching, making their noises. You know how noisy humans can be. Sorry. You're so quiet I forget you are a human.

Netherby did not understand human words. He only knew they came from humans. Some of the words rumbled, some squirted above the rumble, others churned on so fast there were hardly any spaces between them. He didn't know what they meant but he knew by how loud they were that the humans were close. Netherby gave Newt a sharp elbow in the side.

"Go to work."

Newt sat up bleary-eyed. He had forgotten where he was, what his mission was supposed to be, even that he was a Gnarly. "Oh, yes," he said, finally remembering he was a Gnarly, that he was in South Woods, that he was on a mission to confound humans. Then, after another moment, "What am I supposed to do?"

"A call," rasped Netherby. "A call that will raise the hackles on the humans' hide. A call that will make their bones rattle. A call that will chase them out of South Woods, across the stone wall and back into the Way-Way Yonda where they belong!"

Newt rubbed his eyes. Blinked. "I thought we were just going to have fun with humans."

"We are on a mission," Netherby said with a little hop. "Our greatest mission ever. To rid North Woods and South Woods of humans forever!"

"No more gooble?" asked Nodwart.

"There will be gooble," sighed Netherby. "But on the other side of the stone wall."

"But humans aren't afraid of anything," Newt argued.

"Everything is afraid of something."

"But what? And how does it sound?" Newt shuffled his invisible deck of cards. His green eyes were as big as they could get.

Netherby now regretted that he had not thought his plan through a little more carefully. He searched through his memory for something terrifying enough to scare humans.

"Dragons. That's it. Make a dragon sound!"

Newt was lost. He shuffled his cards faster as he tried to imagine what a dragon was. He had heard something about dragons—or was it dinosaurs?—in lore, but that was a long time ago. He looked at Nodwart for help, but of course, Nodwart had no idea either.

"Just do it!" roared Netherby.

Newt shot back an angry look, the look an artist gives to those who do not understand that art does not happen on command. Art is a gift. Sometimes you have to wait for it to come to you; sometimes if you ask, it will come, but only in its own time.

This, of course, drives Netherby to fits. He does not have the patience that art calls for. He stormed back and forth, twirled his scarf, jabbed his lance into the ground. But he said nothing. He knew that it would do no good.

Newt, in the meantime, clasped his busy hands together and settled down to concentrate on his juju.

He collected himself into a little ball and stretched out his neck. The tuft of fur between his ears rose up like a rooster's comb, then flattened, then rose again. Netherby hopped up and down, waiting for a sound to emerge. Newt, despite the urgency, seemed in no hurry. He was in a trance. There were long moments of silence as he dug deeper and deeper into his juju for the sound of a dragon.

What he delivered was dragonless.

It was a song. The notes so poignant they brought Nodwart to tears, then to loud snuffles that had to be shushed. The notes lifted into the air, then sifted down through the woods in a crystal waterfall of sound. It was the wrong sound, of course, but Newt was so dazzled by it his eyes closed in rapture.

"Again, with the wood thrush!" snapped Netherby. "Where's the blood-curdling screech? The fire?"

Newt hung his head. The wood thrush song had come even though he was thinking dragon. The problem was, he didn't know what a dragon sounded like. "I only know what I hear," he said dismally.

"Then make it up! Use your imagination!"

The humans would have passed by then, but they had stopped to look at something through their binoculars.

"Imagine dragons. Big, flying, fiery. Imagine dinosaurs. Earth-shaking big. Throw some mosquitoes in there, too." It occurred to Netherby that the one thing he had seen capable of driving humans from the woods were swarms of mosquitoes.

The Gnarlys watched from behind the grasses as the humans started to walk away again. Newt became anxious as he tried to think up a sound that would contain all the things Netherby said before the humans got too far away.

He balled up his body even tighter and rounder, turned his head a little to the side and let out a sound that could only be described as a cross between a mink frog and a coyote, with a hint of mosquito, if you can imagine such a thing.

It was good, all right, even though it didn't contain a single dragon or dinosaur. To Newt's dismay, the humans talked right over it. This made Newt's tuft flatten with anger. He took great pride in his juju.

Netherby looked over at him expectantly. Nodwart shook his head and yawned as if the whole thing had been a big disappointment.

Newt could not let the humans get away with ignoring him. He scrunched up his face and turned a reddish hue that shone right through his gray fur. His tiny round ears and nose burned bright red, too. He puffed up his body so you could hardly see his head at all. Then, when the humans were almost out of sight, he let loose a sound that stunned the other two Gnarlys, silenced every other sound in the woods, and stopped the humans in their tracks.

It was a sound the likes of which had never been heard in North Woods, South Woods, the east, or the west. In fact, maybe not in this entire universe. Remember when I said that even Newt didn't know how much juju he had? Well, the sound he made surprised him more than anyone else. It wasn't dragon or dinosaur or mosquito and certainly not wood thrush. It was a sound that must have swooped through him out of another world.

Netherby was speechless. Nodwart, as usual, baffled. The humans did not utter a sound for a few moments.

When they spoke, Newt was pleased with the awe that rung through their voices.

"Was that . . . could it be . . . a great crested albatross?!"

"It sounded like . . . a bay-breasted bottom-snatcher to me," said the other.

"That's impossible. They only inhabit the rain forests of Borneo."

Both humans swung their binoculars in all directions, scanning thickets and treetops searching for whatever had made the unearthly sound.

Newt, excited by the reaction he had gotten from his call, repeated it, this time adding a hissing sound at the end.

The humans dropped their binoculars and hit the ground.

"It's right on top of us! Duck!" The humans sprawled on the ground and covered their heads with their hands. Then, as Newt let the sound trail away, they looked up, then at each other. They were speechless, which is unusual for humans.

"Whatever made that call could be the find of a lifetime," one of them whispered when the sound had almost died away.

"*If* we can find it!" said the other.

Newt, hopping up and down with glee, made the sound come back again. This time it swooped even lower, then continued for a long time, like the albatross or bottom-snatcher was circling overhead. The humans scrambled to their feet. Still half crouching, they peered off over the treetops, jabbering excitedly to each other, then hurried back the way they had come. Their words no longer rushed together, but dropped lower, with more spaces between them, as if the humans were carrying a valuable secret away with them.

"Well, that's that," said Nodwart, who was growing a little bored with the humans. "Aha," he said, brightening. He scurried over to a pink glob that had been left on the trail. "Gooble!" he exclaimed in delight.

Newt was too caught up in his sound making to notice. It was hard to stop him once he got started. Netherby had to take hold of his shoulders and shake him several times.

Birds were beginning to gather, chipping sharp warnings. They knew only a Gnarly could make such a call, and Gnarlys always meant trouble.

Netherby was delighted. His plan had worked! The humans had been driven from South Woods back into the Way-Way Yonda. It was his new masterwork. "Let's find something to celebrate the Gnomes down a hole and the humans back in the Way-Way Yonda!" he sang out, twirling his scarf.

"Like eat," said Nodwart. "Nodwart hungry."

The vision of the cozy den still Gnome-free and with more dried fruits and berries, pollen cakes, acorns, and honeycomb to plunder flashed through the mind of each Gnarly.

"I know just the place," said Netherby, rubbing his hands together. With Netherby leading the way—as if he knew the way—Nodwart clutching the wad of gooble, and Newt still dazed by his tour de force, the Gnarlys set off for the Gnomes' den and found it quite by accident.

They ate as much as they could, then stuffed their rucklesacks with pollen cakes, dried mushrooms, and berries to take back to their own gruf.

They were so overloaded with booty and so tired from the day's events they could not quite climb the hill to their gruf, so they crawled under the cap of a toppled parasol mushroom and fell asleep just downhill of Sweet Fat Mama.

Newt couldn't sleep though. With Nodwart's croak and Netherby's snort and whistle joining the chorus of the katydids, Newt thought about his work of art, the sound he had made for the humans. He was very proud of it and yet he knew he could have made it even better. Then the humans would have stayed and amused the Gnarlys a little longer looking scared and confused, and maybe dropping something even better than gooble that the Gnarlys could take back to Sweet Fat Mama and add to their collection.

Then Newt stopped thinking about the sound and fell asleep.

Field Note

—

Gnarlys are big collectors. They especially like to gather items that might be used in one of their traps, decoys, or catapults. Gnarlys find items discarded by humans especially useful for these purposes.

—

Chapter Twelve

Gnomes on the Rampage

⟿⟿

WHILE the Gnarlys slept under the mushroom cap, their bellies full of spoils from the Gnomes' den, the Gnomes were beginning to think maybe they should find out how serious the early snowstorm was.

If the Gnarlys had thought things out a little further, it might have occurred to them that the Gnomes would soon investigate the situation. It is not the Gnomes' nature to let Nature take its course. Gnomes think that Nature must be reminded, from time to time, to keep on task. They were not likely to sit and wait for the early winter to pass.

"I'm going up," announced the Foolish Gnome to the others who were crowded around *How Nature Works,* trying to read in the dim light of the hole. "That's the only way to tell how deep the snow is."

"And just what's going on up there," said the Wisest Gnome who was one step behind the Foolish Gnome in suspecting a Gnarly behind the early winter.

Even the Nubbins were beginning to catch on. There was something very Gnarly-like about this sudden appearance of winter. The Just-in-Case burrow they had clambered into to escape the sudden storm lacked the usual store of supplies. While the Gnomes were quite content to do without, the Nubbins were growing grouchy. The Just-in-Case was meant to be a quick refuge from storms, such as an early winter storm, or as an escape hatch from owls or hawks or worse, crows or humans. Unlike most Gnome burrows, or the burrows of animals that use underground passageways (moles, voles, chipmunks, and so on) there was no other way out.

This burrow happened to be an especially steep drop, so the Gnomes were forced to form a Gnome ladder to lift one another out. The problem was, the Wisest Gnome (whom the Nubbins called the Fattest—just to one another, of course) insisted on being the first to climb out, which meant he had to be hoisted up on top of the others, where he squatted on the head of the Gnome under him, who balanced on the shoulders of the Gnome under him and so on. The Wisest (and, yes, fattest) sat for a long time out of breath at the top of the pile, his bulk squashing hats, dislocating noses, and bending backs. The Gnomes below gasped and grunted and began to grumble unkind remarks.

"*Boulderdazzlefrumpcake!*" thundered down from the Wisest Gnome on top to the most squashed Nubbins on the bottom of the pile. As the Wisest attempted to uncover the entrance to the burrow, he shifted his considerable weight this way and that way until the Gnomes below could no longer support him and the pile collapsed in a heap at the bottom of the burrow.

Down tumbled the Wisest on top of the other Gnomes with milkweed silk drifting down overall.

"Gnarlys!" roared the Foolish Gnome.

"Gnarlys!" repeated the others.

Gnomes are usually orderly. Gnomes are usually respectful. But these Gnomes were so angry they scrambled out of the hole like raging ground bees, every Gnome for himself.

"*Habblesnark rumblejuice!*" roared the Wisest Gnome, still trapped down the hole. The others hurried back to retrieve him, though the Wisest kicked and flailed and fumed so violently they lost several minutes trying to extract him.

"Thunderbombs! Whittlesticks!" roared the enraged Wisest Gnome as he finally popped out of the hole, pulling milkweed silk out of his hair, his nose, and his shockingly red ears.

With all the Gnomes out of the hole and the Wisest huffing furiously in the lead, they stalked the woods for Gnarlys.

Field Note

The Gnome's Just-in-Case holes range from those that are well prepared with chambers and exit tunnels and stores of food to those that are just for emergencies—for diving in out of harm's way. Gnarlys, animals, and amphibians make use of the Gnomes' Just-in-Case holes for the same purpose.

Chapter Thirteen

Humans Everywhere!

❧

THE Gnarlys had no idea what they had set in motion. After being evicted from under the mushroom cap by a foraging raccoon, they slipped down one of their tunnels leading into *Sweet Fat Mama* to continue their sleep and happy dreams. They were snoozing soundly, Netherby's snore of snorts and whistles alternating with Nodwart's croak, punctuated by Newt's trilling song. Snugly cocooned within mounds of cattail silk and clouds of thistledown, they did not stir until a very large noise shook the bark of *Sweet Fat Mama* and interrupted the pattern of snores.

Netherby was the first to awaken. Gnarlys do not snap to alertness like other creatures of the forest, and for a few minutes he stood at the entrance of the gruf rubbing his eyes, scratching his belly, grumbling, snorting, coughing, and watching things go from fuzzy to terrifying.

Then he shot back into the recesses of the gruf.

"Humans!" he shouted. "Humans everywhere!"

The other two sputtered awake.

"Humans?" Newt asked in disbelief. "In our forest?"

Humans on the trail, even humans in South Woods, were very different from humans in North Woods. Netherby couldn't stop nodding his head. His eyes were so wide the whites shown all around the bobbing black irises. He pressed himself into the shadows of Sweet Fat Mama as if he hoped to become part of the tree. Then he curled up into a ball of fur.

Newt and Nodwart stared at him in alarm. They had never seen Netherby frightened before. Even when he was, it was hidden behind the swish of his scarf, the thrust of his lance. The other two Gnarlys huddled close together on the opposite side of the gruf and gazed in wonder at the little fur ball that had been their leader only a few hours ago.

You're surprised, too? After all, Netherby *was* the one with the big idea to chase the humans back into the Way-Way Yonda. Well, something happened inside Netherby's mind when he saw so many humans in North Woods. A memory returned like a bad dream.

It was in his home forest, Woods of the White Pines, where Netherby first saw humans. They came into the forest in great numbers and made war on the trees. They brought down every one, then broke them into pieces, including the ancient pine which was the gruf of Netherby and his family.

The destruction of their home came so swiftly that the confused and panicked Gnarlys fled down the closest escape tunnels they could find, each emerging in a different part of the ravaged forest, each having to find their way alone. The memory brought back to Netherby the shock of finding himself alone in the broken forest among the stunned silence of birds, the wide sky staring down on him.

It was all like a terrible dream, but Netherby knew what had happened to his forest was no dream. He knew that it could happen to North Woods just as it happened to Woods of the White Pine. He knew without trees, there would be no beechnuts to eat, no birds to mimic. No Gnomes to aggravate. No Sweet Fat Mama. No Gnarlys.

~⊚~

Newt could not bear to gaze upon the little ball of fear that had been their leader. He pulled Nodwart to his feet and the two tiptoed toward Netherby. Newt knelt down in front of the Gnarly leader, though he couldn't tell what was Netherby's beginning and what was his end.

"Netherby," he said in a hopeful voice, "let's show those Gnomes!" There was no response from Netherby. "Hi-ho a Merry-O, the Gnomes down a hole," he sang to the roundness before him. Newt searched for other inspiring words that might snap Netherby out of roundness. "Take your positions," he demanded. Still, nothing.

A thunder cracking sound shook Sweet Fat Mama.

"Timber!" cried Nodwart.

Netherby sprung to attention. His eyes darted back and forth. He looked even more Netherby-like than he had before. Swinging his scarf around his neck, he dashed to the entrance of the gruf, then dove out of sight to one side. He motioned the other two over. Newt and Nodwart crawled on their bellies to the other side of the entrance. All three peered out into the forest.

North Woods swarmed with humans. Humans big, humans small, humans with hats, humans without hats, humans with strange contraptions hanging from their necks and middles, humans looking up and humans looking down, and all of them talking, talking, talking.

"Humans!" was all Netherby managed to say. All three Gnarlys gazed in terror at the scene before them.

Humans were so close the Gnarlys could see their faces, contorted with concentration.

"What do they want?" asked Newt, shuffling his invisible deck of cards.

"With humans, you never know," replied Netherby. "But we have to do something fast or . . ."

"Or what?" asked the other two in unison.

"With humans, you never know," was all Netherby said. He frowned and backed away again, into the recesses of Sweet Fat Mama.

"Aha," said Nodwart. "They want gooble back."

"No," Netherby sighed. "It's more than gooble."

"Maybe they want our pine nuts," offered Newt.

Netherby shook his head. "Humans want bigger things than gooble and nuts. They never want anything small." But even Netherby couldn't come up with why the humans were searching through the woods, looking up and down, opening books, and peering through binoculars, talking, talking,

talking. How had his plan to chase humans out of the woods brought them farther into the woods?

"Back!" shouted Netherby, and the Gnarlys flattened against the back of the gruf.

A human as tall as a sapling, wearing tree shadow hues, appeared directly in front of the Gnarly gruf. He bent down and peered inside the entrance. Everything went black inside Sweet Fat Mama. Then another human came and looked in, too. The Gnarlys could not make out the features of the humans, only the up and down of their voices.

The humans couldn't see the Gnarlys flattened in the shadows on either side of the entrance, but the Gnarlys feared the thumping of their hearts against the tree would certainly be heard. To their relief, the humans detected nothing. They stood up and again looked up and down the great tree. All this time they were talking in voices that went low and high, high and low.

Inside, the Gnarlys tried to hold their breath and any terrified squeaks that might escape from their throats. They had never been so frightened. It took all their effort not to curl up into three little balls of fur. It was the first time fear had reached them inside their gruf.

They realized, then, that even inside Sweet Fat Mama, the largest tree in the forest, they were not safe from everything.

The traps and barricades they had constructed to thwart marauding Gnomes, raccoons, and squirrels, were nothing against humans. In fact, the humans who poked their noses inside Sweet Fat Mama hardly noticed the pots of pine sap that spilled upon their boots or the drop holes their boots sank into.

Humans prowling around Sweet Fat Mama had destroyed all but a few of the Gnarlys' secret tunneling systems leading into and out of their gruf.

The Gnarlys pressed close together in the darkness of the tree. They could hear the humans' voices running up and down, stopping, starting, then suddenly accelerating. Then, the thrashing of brush and crunching of acorns and twigs. Several humans seemed to be gathering around Sweet Fat Mama.

"They are going to take Sweet Fat Mama down!" gasped Netherby. "They will break her into pieces." Netherby was losing his Netherby-ness again. His fear swept through the others.

"Then all the trees will go!" they exclaimed together in whispered panic. They listened as hard as they could. The woods thrashed and the ground trembled in the way that said humans were upon it.

"We could make a run for it," suggested Newt. "Out one of the tunnels. The humans won't even see us." There was a long silence while the other two Gnarlys thought this over.

"Where Gnarlys go?" asked Nodwart after a while. At these words, Netherby thought of his lost, scattered family, none of whom he had ever seen again. None of the Gnarlys could imagine life outside of Sweet Fat Mama and North Woods.

While Netherby paced, trying to gather his courage again, Newt shuffled his invisible cards, and Nodwart stood open-mouthed in wonder, the woods went abruptly silent. Like a storm had passed or paused. Newt crept to the entrance. There wasn't a single human. He sighed in relief and crept back to the other Gnarlys. "They're gone!" he exclaimed.

"For now," said Netherby.

"What do we do if they come back?" asked Newt.

Nodwart, who could not stand another dew drop of excitement, collapsed in a heap of exhaustion on a pile of thistledown at the far end of the gruf.

"We'll sleep on it," Netherby answered at last.

꩜

Most episodes in a Gnarly's life are forgotten as soon as it is time for a nap or meal, but not this one. The Gnarlys could not sleep and could not eat. They knew the humans would return, and they were right.

The next morning there were even more of them. They prowled the forest, whacking through the underbrush and saplings with their own kind of whittlesticks. Then they sat as silently as humans can for long periods of time up against trees. Two sat against Sweet Fat Mama, one blocking the entrance to the Gnarly gruf.

"We have to do something fast," Netherby whispered. The other two could barely see him in the little bit of light that came through the gruf. They watched his dark form as he paced, thrusting his lance in and out of the light. They were sure one of Netherby's big ideas was soon to emerge, but nothing did.

Finally, Netherby stopped pacing. Newt and Nodwart leaned forward, ready to hear the plan. Netherby gave a hop and one last jab in the air with his lance. "We need help," he announced.

Nodwart and Newt looked at each other, then back at Netherby. They were glad that Netherby had come up with an idea, but this did not seem like a good one.

Who could the Gnarlys ask for help in North Woods? They were on the birds' Most Wanted list for the hundreds of times the Gnarlys had switched their eggs and fooled them with hawk calls. The deer would stomp on them in an instant, the red and gray squirrels would be happy to see the woods free of acorn-stealing Gnarlys, and the bees would swarm them for all the times they had raided their honey. Even the docile frogs and newts and toads had complaints of their own against the Gnarlys. And the . . .

"Gnomes," said Netherby almost under his breath.

"Gnomes?!" inquired Newt, stepping forward.

"Gnomes," Netherby repeated a little louder.

"Ask a Gnome for help?" piped Newt. "We have never, never, never asked a Gnome for help."

"Whittlesticks and thunderbombs." added Nodwart, "and hot, puffy breath."

"Gnomes and Gnarlys are rivals," reasoned Newt. "For centuries. It's tradition. We can't break tradition."

Netherby was uncharacteristically silent while the other two Gnarlys' complaints buzzed around him like the frenzy of bees that had just been raided. He did not usually let Newt and Nodwart get so many words out, but he was deep in his own thoughts.

Netherby knew his plan was against Nature. It was against the Gnarly nature to ask a Gnome for help. It was against a Gnome's nature to help a Gnarly, especially Gnomes who had just been tricked once again by Gnarlys. But he also knew the situation called for something bigger than the long-standing rivalry.

"Besides," Newt said, breaking through Netherby's thoughts. "How can Gnomes help? They only know what's in *How Nature Works*."

"Humans not Nature," added Nodwart.

Then both Nodwart and Newt shook their heads and said in unison: "No Gnomes." The two stood facing Netherby, their jaws set in determination.

"Yes. Gnomes," said Netherby calmly. "It's our only hope."

Though Nodwart and Newt grumbled their complaints, Netherby knew they would end up following whatever plan he came up with, even if it was against Nature. The problem was, he did not know how the Gnomes could help or if anything could. But he didn't tell the other Gnarlys that.

After a while, the humans moved on to South Woods, but Netherby assured the other two they would return, and probably with more humans.

"Uniforms are called for," Netherby announced once the humans were out of sight. "And lances." The other two Gnarlys began assembling their beetle wings and beechnut husk helmets and fetching their lances from their secret chamber deep inside Sweet Fat Mama.

Field Note

None of the Gnarlys were born in North Woods. They all came from other forests that lost their trees to loggers or to human constructions. Only Netherby remembers his exodus. Newt and Nodwart were deposited in North Woods by crows—for reasons only a crow knows—when they were too young to remember.

Chapter Fourteen

Gnarlys and Gnomes Together?

✺

T wouldn't be hard for the Gnarlys to find the Gnomes since the Gnomes were looking for the Gnarlys. The troop of Gnomes and Nubbins carried thunderbombs in their rucklesacks and hoisted their whittlesticks. They intended to drive the Gnarlys as far from North Woods as they could chase them, even if it took days.

These were very, very angry Gnomes. Gnomes, you see, do not like to be made fools of, and the Gnarlys never cease to put them in some sort of embarrassing situation. It makes the Gnomes especially angry when it appears they do not know as much as they think they know about how Nature works. The false winter was the last puff. Finding their den in shambles was the puff after the last puff.

"You should have known," grumbled the Oldest Gnome to the Wisest Gnome as they bushwhacked through a stand of club moss atop a small boulder, "that there was a Gnarly behind this. Winter never comes *this* early. How could you have been so fooled?"

"And what about yourself!" returned the Wisest. "You are the Oldest, after all. Haven't your years taught you anything?"

"There is no good to come of fighting each other," said the Foolish Gnome. "Save your fight for Gnarlys."

The Gnomes fell silent and concentrated on their expedition to the Gnarly gruf. They could not help but look up at the bright blue skies and sunlight pouring through leaves tinged with red and gold, shake their heads and wonder how they could have been so fooled.

~ॐ~

The Gnomes knew very well that the Gnarly gruf was inside Sweet Fat Mama but knowing was not enough.

They dared not approach the giant maple that towered over Highbush Hill, though the opening at her base was wide and welcoming. The Gnarlys had an excellent view of the forest from inside the giant tree and had devised an elaborate system of booby traps for unwelcome guests. It was next to impossible to catch a Gnarly coming and going from the gruf because they used an underground network of tunnels.

The Gnomes did not know that the human invasion destroyed much of the Gnarly defense system and had collapsed most of the tunnels. They had an advantage this time, though. The Gnarlys thought they were still tucked safely down a hole, waiting out the winter.

∽◉◦

The sun had already begun its westward descent by the time the Gnomes crept to just downhill of Sweet Fat Mama.

"Those nasty little furballs are in there right now sleeping off a feast of our winter stores," grumbled the Oldest Gnome.

Their plan was to catch the dozy Gnarlys unaware as they stumbled out to catch the afternoon sun before returning to the booty from the Gnomes' larder; that is if they hadn't already fallen into their post-feast slumber, which was known to go on for days. If so, the Gnomes were determined to wait it out. They settled into a hollowed-out log with a good view of the entrance to the gruf.

Unlike Gnarlys, Gnomes are patient. They can wait and watch for days, if necessary. The Gnarlys, however, were not home. As you know, they were on a mission of their own—to find the Gnomes.

∽◉◦

Of course, the Gnomes were not where the Gnarlys thought, either.

"Looks like they don't have to be rescued after all." The Gnarlys peered down into the Just-in-Case hole that the Gnomes had furiously vacated upon discovering that the early winter was instead a false winter brought on by nothing more than Gnarlys. Milkweed silk wafted over the ground in front of the hole. It had been shredded into tiny pieces by angry Gnome hands.

"Hmm. They could be anywhere," said Netherby, stroking his chin fur and looking around the woods, as if a Gnome might pop up behind them at any moment.

"They are probably off doing something Gnomish," offered Newt. "Like inspecting toad warts or counting midges."

"Or . . . looking for Gnarlys," said Netherby. "Gnomes don't like tricks if you recall. Gnomes have a very small sense of humor."

"Small as a chigger," said Newt

"Small as a . . . ," started Nodwart, but he couldn't think of anything.

"They're going to be hopping mad," said Netherby. The thought of hopping mad Gnomes inspired Nodwart, who began to hop. Netherby and Newt hooted in laughter at the thought of hopping mad Gnomes and the sight of Nodwart with his huge feet flapping.

After Nodwart tripped over his feet on the last hop, the Gnarlys decided they should return to Sweet Fat Mama and have a thought about the situation.

There was a lot to think about. It occurred to Netherby along the way that hopping mad Gnomes were not likely to listen to a Gnarly plan. The first thing on their minds would probably be running Gnarlys out of the woods. The last thing on their minds would be helping Gnarlys.

Netherby was so busy thinking about the problem of the Gnomes that he almost led the Gnarlys straight into them. Just before entering the hollow log that was a frequently used Gnarly shortcut to one of the tunnels leading into Sweet Fat Mama, he detected the tips of whittlesticks protruding from a dark lumpiness inside the log.

"Sweet birch!" he gasped. "Our log has Gnome stuffing."

The Gnarlys could read the anger all bunched up inside the dark figures of the hunkering Gnomes.

"I don't think they are going to listen to your plan," whispered Newt.

"We'll just have to make them listen, won't we?" said Netherby." He ushered the two back under a bunchberry. "Here's what we do . . ."

∽๑๐

In less time than it takes a Gnome to say *rumblesnarkle-frumplesnock* five times, the Gnarlys had raided enough abandoned spider webs to compile a hefty bundle of webbing. Gnarlys, who can raise more noise than a bellowing moose, can also be as quiet as fog rolling in.

While the Gnomes peered intently in the direction of the Gnarly gruf entrance, the Gnarlys were laying a trap behind them.

Once the trap was set, Netherby appeared at the end of the log in back of the Gnomes, hands on hips, helmet set at a jaunty angle, scarf just so.

"Well, if it isn't the Gnomes," he chortled. "Lovely weather we're having after all."

The bundle of Gnomes turned at once. Their fury could be felt through the spider web that stretched between themselves and Netherby.

"*GurRUMP, bongdoodle, snarkwaddle,*" snorted the Gnomes as they scrambled over one another in their rage to get at the

Gnarly who taunted them from the other end of the hollow log. Unable to see the webbing in the fading light of the day, they burst out of the log in one big ball of angry Gnomes and were instantly ensnared in a thick net of spider web.

The ball of web with furious Gnomes inside bounced over the ground for a while, whittlesticks stabbing through it and spores puffing out of it.

The webbing was so thick, and the Gnomes so crowded together it was hard for the Gnarlys to understand a single word that came out of the ball of spider web. Just a *snorkel* here, a *snittledoom* there.

When the ball finally quit bouncing, and the grumbling and shouts died down to pants and squeaks, Netherby spoke.

"Settle down Gnomes and listen to reason. This is not a Gnarly trick."

The ball of web went silent. Thunderbomb spores choked the air.

"We had no choice but to web you," said Netherby. "Indeed, it was the only way we could get you to listen to reason. Okay, okay, we know you may be a little, indeed, grumpy about that last . . . incident."

The web ball coughed, thumped, and growled.

"But this is not a trick. Indeed." A short pause. "We have a proposal for you, Gnomes. A proposition. We have tended to find ourselves in a befuddlement." Netherby puffed up his chest to hold all the big words he thought he needed for the situation.

Nodwart, who had fewer words to get in the way, said simply, "We have humans."

Netherby scowled at Nodwart. "I was just going to say . . . yes . . . humans." He cleared his throat. "They have created a *jeopardious* situation . . ."

"Too many," interrupted Nodwart.

"Yes," said Netherby, his chest deflating. "Too many."

"We need help," said Newt.

"*Gnome* help," Nodwart added.

At this, the ball of web thumped and growled louder.

"It's true," said Netherby excitedly. "There are humans every-where. Something got them all stirred up and now they are off the path and all over North and South Woods. You know how dangerous humans can be once they get off the path. They'll trample everything. They'll cut down our trees. Then no more Gnarlys. And no more *Gnomes*."

There were more sounds mixed with coughing inside the web, but the Gnarlys couldn't tell what any of it meant. After some discussion among themselves, they decided to free the Gnomes and take their chances. First, of course, they removed all the whittlesticks protruding from the web, then they un-wound the web bit by bit.

Finally, there was a heap of Gnomes on the forest floor along with two Nubbins, all choking on a cloud of spores.

"We need a plan," said Netherby breathlessly. "Using your *great* organizational skills and our juju we can run those hu-mans out of the woods forever! But we have to work together."

"Indeed!" snarled the Foolish Gnome sarcastically as he wobbled to his feet. He squinted one bleary eye at the Gnarlys. "And we should believe you?!"

"Indeed," answered Netherby with much less certainty.

As the Gnomes began to revive, the Gnarlys could see they were not going to be in an agreeable frame of mind.

The mass of green jackets, red pants, and crushed red caps began to separate from one another, revealing furiously flushed cheeks and noses and beady blue eyes aimed at the Gnarlys like bullets. Even without whittlesticks or thunderbombs, the Gnomes were a fearsome looking bunch.

"Run for it!" shouted Newt.

But just at that moment, as the Gnarlys were poised to flee and the Gnomes poised to chase, the ground shook, a shadow loomed overhead and the earth beside them was struck by a huge object, missing the Gnomes and Gnarlys by inches. Dragging pieces of spider web and leaving lances and whittlesticks behind, the Gnomes and Gnarlys fled in the same direction—for the safety of Sweet Fat Mama.

With the defense system collapsed, the entrance to Sweet Fat Mama was welcoming, even to the Gnomes.

Field Note

The Gnarly tunnels are also used to trap intruders. The tunnel will start out large enough to accommodate say, a Gnome, but then shrink down to Gnarly size so that the intruder cannot proceed and if he tries to back out, he will most surely be met with the point of a Gnarly lance or be caught up in a Gnarly net.

Chapter Fifteen

An Occasion of Historic Proportions

∽✺∾

NEVER in all the years there had been Gnarlys and Gnomes in North Woods were there ever Gnomes and Gnarlys in the same gruf at the same time in North Woods. But there they were on this occasion of historic proportions, three Gnarlys, three Gnomes, and two Nubbins inside Sweet Fat Mama, all together, and all breathing very hard from narrowly escaping being crushed by humans.

The Gnomes and Gnarlys clustered on opposite sides of the trunk. The Gnomes glared at the Gnarlys for a while, then looked around the gruf, appalled by the disarray.

The gruf was littered with various forms of bedding—thistledown, tufts of moss, mats of horsetail, cattail fluff, and cotton grass—along with sundry items collected from field and forest, such as pine cones, bird feathers, mushrooms, milkweed pods, dried grasses, oak apple galls, and beetle wings.

Adding to the clutter were many found items collected from the humans' trail and which the Gnarlys hoped to put to use—empty shell casings, coins, the foil from candy bar wrappers, bottle caps, a bottle opener, elastic hair ties, wads of gooble, cellophane, a penknife, and a Smartphone which had baffled the Gnarlys for two years.

There were also Gnarly projects in various stages of completion using some of these found objects—several pointed implements, including a straightened paperclip to drill sap from Sweet Fat Mama and the yellow birch, a sling-shot fashioned from rubber bands, and a basket-like trap woven from strips of plastic. The Gnomes could only guess at the purposes of these various contraptions.

Nowhere in the chaos of the Gnarly gruf did they see neatly stacked supplies of dried fruits, acorns, beechnuts, pollen cakes, or honey tubs for the winter, or beeswax lanterns. The only remnants of food were scraps and crumbs from the raid on the Gnomes' den, scattered about the gruf and stuck to the fur of the Gnarlys. Occasionally, a Gnarly would pick a piece of pollen cake from his fur and chew on it while warily watching the Gnomes across the gruf.

"How do you Gnarlys survive the winter?" asked the Wisest in obvious distaste.

"They steal from us," grunted the Oldest. The other Gnomes began to grumble among themselves at this. A chirp of laughter escaped from a Nubbin.

"Now let's not get off on the wrong foot," offered Netherby. "Nestle down in a clump of cushy and make yourselves comfy."

"Not Newt's," snapped Newt, pulling a pillow of thistledown from under a Nubbin who had already made himself very comfortable.

Netherby flung a piece of acorn at Newt. He was trying very hard, perhaps *too* hard, to gain the Gnomes' support for his plan. "This is an occasion of historic proportions," he continued. "Gnomes and Gnarlys saving the forest from humans."

None of the others seemed to share Netherby's sense of occasion. The Gnomes, refusing all comforts, kicked aside the cattail fluff at their feet and squatted on the bare earth of Sweet Fat Mama, looking with contempt upon the dark recesses and clutter of the gruf.

Newt and Nodwart sat upon their cloud of thistledown and gazed with equal contempt at the Gnomes. Between them, in a shaft of sunlight that had slipped in through the tree's cavity, Netherby struck a pose as if he were about to conduct an orchestra.

Netherby was less confident than he appeared to be. Gnomes, even without whittlesticks and thunderbombs, are a threat to Gnarlys. They are three times the size and outnumber the Gnarlys five to three. Netherby knew that at any moment the Gnomes might overpower the Gnarlys and claim Sweet Fat Mama for their own.

But as the last light of the setting sun leaked across the floor of the gruf, the Gnomes looked less threatening than grumpy. They were also more concerned, for the moment at least, with the human invasion, a far greater threat to the forest than the scourge of Gnarlys.

"Do you think the humans saw us?" asked a Nubbin.

Though the Wisest opened his mouth to speak, the Foolish Gnome spoke first. "No," he answered. "Humans only see what they're looking for and they don't know they are looking for us."

Netherby was the only one who understood what the Foolish Gnome meant. He began to pace in a little circle between the Gnomes and the Gnarlys. He was thinking very, very hard. Then he gave a hop and turned to the Gnomes.

"Gnomes think they . . . Gnomes *know* . . . a lot about how Nature works," he began. The Gnomes looked at him sideways, their pointy-bearded chins raised. "But you also know a lot about how humans work," continued Netherby.

"Humans?" snorted the Oldest. "Humans aren't part of Nature. How would we know anything about humans?"

"Because Gnomes are . . . a kind of human," said Netherby, growing less and less certain of the direction he seemed to be taking. The Gnomes' faces grew redder. "Wee, wee, wee humans, of course," said Netherby, taking a step back.

"We are Gnomes!" roared the Oldest, who had eased himself down to rest on the remains of a paper wasp's nest, and now rose to his feet with some difficulty. There was a glint of amusement in the Foolish Gnomes' eyes if anyone were to notice. He was enjoying watching Netherby talk himself into a trap.

"But . . . look at you," Netherby squeaked, taking two more steps backward. He glanced over at Nodwart and Newt for support but the two gazed at him with the same rapt expression they had when watching a spider spin a fly into its web.

Netherby turned back to the surly Gnome faces. He was speaking very quickly now. "You have no fur except on your head and over your eyes, and a little sprouting from your pointy chin and ears. And you have the same knobs on your faces that humans do." Netherby took a deep breath. "And you cover yourselves in the same way!" There was a thunderous moment of silence. "Wondrously so, I might add," he finished in a high, wobbly voice.

"Wondrously?" Nodwart turned to Newt, who shrugged his shoulders. A squeak of laughter spurted from a Nubbin.

The Gnomes seemed to like the word, though. They looked down at their jackets and pants and boots. Gnomes are very proud of the bright clothing that they weave out of rabbit fur and dye with extract of lichen, bloodroot, and rushes.

"And you make fire!" This was the one skill the Gnomes had borrowed from Nature that most amazed the Gnarlys. They could make fire out of cattail spikes. Even as Netherby said the word, "fire" the other two Gnarlys bowed their heads, briefly, in deference to the Gnomes. Fire was magic to the Gnarlys. The only juju that the Gnomes had ever made.

After acknowledging Gnome superiority with a clearing of throats and nods to one another, the Oldest Gnome gathered himself and glared at the Gnarlys. "But Gnomes are Gnomes!" he shouted.

"Gnomes are Gnomes!" the Foolish Gnome shouted, even louder.

"Gnomes are Gnomes!" barked the Wisest, adding an emphatic nod of his head.

"Gnomes are Gnomes!" giggled the Nubbins.

Netherby threw up his hands in defeat. "Gnomes are Gnomes," he sighed and plopped down glumly between the two groups. The sun had retreated from the center of the floor and now rested on the feet of the Gnomes.

Perhaps it was the warmth of the sun settling on the Gnomes, or perhaps it was the word "wondrously," or the flattery about fire making, but slowly the Wisest turned from outraged to thoughtful.

"Of course," he said, taking off his red cap and scratching his mat of white hair, "you could say humans *were* a kind of Gnome. Before they got called away by the unnatural world." The Wisest glanced about Sweet Fat Mama and the odd assortment of human-made objects strewn across the floor. "I see Gnarlys have a fascination for the unnatural world, too," he said. The Nubbins chuckled behind him. It was a few moments before the Wisest regained his train of thought. He twirled his cap in his hands while the words gathered.

"*How Nature Works* tells it all," he continued, encouraged by an audience. "The natural part of humans was left with the Gnomes for safe keeping." The light stood now at the entrance of the gruf as if waiting to hear the Wisest Gnome's words before departing. The other Gnomes muttered and nodded to one another in agreement.

"The Gnomes take care of all the things that humans left behind when they got called by the unnatural world. It's a big responsibility," said the Wisest, staring accusingly at Netherby, "but somebody has to do it." There was a murmur of agreement from the other Gnomes. The Wisest flipped his cap back on his head and adjusted it to just the right angle. "Of course, that doesn't make a Gnome any less a Gnome," he concluded.

"Of course not," said Netherby with an excited hop. "Now, let us bask in your Gnomliness. Tell us, wondrous Gnomes, what does it take to get humans out of our woods?"

The light had moved out of the gruf. Since the Gnarlys did not have beeswax lanterns or flints to light them with, the group now sat in total darkness. Newt's trill and Nodwart's bullfrog snore soon filled the gruf. The discussion had already gone on too long for them.

Field Note

⎯

Gnomes are known for their orderliness. If a visitor should drop even a crumb of pollen cake on the floor of their den, they might never be invited back.

⎯

—— *Chapter Sixteen* ——

Trouble on Top of Trouble

~⊘~

BEFORE the sun was up the next morning, before the first woodpecker knocked on Sweet Fat Mama, the Gnomes huddled in serious debate at one end of the Gnarly gruf, the tips of their caps pressed together to form a red peak.

The Gnomes' hard thinking awakened the Gnarlys at the other end of the gruf. Even for Netherby, this was too much thinking so early in the morning.

So, while the Gnomes grunted and groaned their serious thoughts to one another, the Gnarlys picked at their toes, rolled over a few times, stared up into the towering blackness of Sweet Fat Mama's trunk, and wondered what was for breakfast.

When the huddle of Gnomes finally broke apart, which might have been minutes or hours later, the Wisest rose to his feet. The other Gnomes rose as well. They were ready to reveal their plan for ridding the woods of humans.

"First," said the Wisest, clearing his throat, "we send a Voped to alert the Gnomes in South Woods and even beyond. We will need a full Gnome army for this challenge."

Netherby did not like the sound of this plan. "Gnome army?"

"Then," continued the Oldest, "we collect thunderbombs, hundreds and hundreds of thunderbombs, and set them off. That will choke the humans and drive them from the forest." The Gnomes were congratulating themselves on their plan, but Netherby looked unimpressed. The other two Gnarlys did not even drop their toes.

"Not big enough," Netherby said with a grave shake of his head.

"Not big enough!? Not big enough for a puny Gnarly, huh?" snorted the Foolish Gnome, advancing toward Netherby. "How about if we give the humans a Gnarly, then, so they will scurry off and study it? Or better—*three* Gnarlys. That will rid the woods of all its problems at once!"

"Not big enough," Netherby repeated, so deep in thought he was unaware of the Foolish Gnome's threatening stance just inches away.

"So, let's hear one of your big ideas, Gnarly!" challenged the Foolish Gnome.

But Netherby could come up with nothing except: "Give them a Gnome. They will soon become bored and wander away."

With a grunt of disdain, the Gnomes returned to one end of the gruf and the Gnarlys to the other. Neither could conjure up a plan big enough because they knew that humans were bigger than any Gnome wisdom or Gnarly trick or juju could match. This led to general grumbling among the unhappy inhabitants of the gruf. The lack of food only made matters worse.

The grumbling quickly turned to insults hurled back and forth along with pieces of dried mushroom, acorn caps, and parts of various Gnarly projects. Soon it was hard to hear above the uproar in the gruf.

The Gnomes, fired up and out of patience, rose up in a Gnome tsunami, advancing on the Gnarlys. But before they could cross the two feet that separated Gnomes from Gnarlys, something even bigger shook Sweet Fat Mama to her roots.

"There's a herd of them!" The Wisest Gnome's voice quaked as he scurried back from the entrance with the terrifying news of another human invasion. "And they have a new kind of monster."

Gnomes and Gnarlys crept over to the entrance. "Dragons!" Newt whispered. The roar of the four-wheeled monster with a human atop, spun over the forest floor, kicking up soil, ferns, and mosses and crushing saplings.

The Wisest Gnome turned to Netherby. Anger was gone. What replaced it was an expression a Gnarly had never seen on the face of a Gnome. For that instant, there was nothing—not years of feuding or trickery or grudges—separating Gnome from Gnarly.

"Our forest. They are crushing our forest!" said the Wisest in despair.

The dragon seemed to be stuck for a moment, then roared free. It sounded like the end of the world was coming.

Gnomes and Gnarlys were struck dumb. Even as the monster sped away—rumbling and crashing down and around Highbush Hill then off toward South Woods—not a word was spoken. As the rumble of the monster grew more distant, another sound rose, though it was even farther away, so far that only the keen hearing of Newt could detect it.

"Crow," he gasped.

The others turned to him with eyes lit with fear. A cold wind had blown into the gruf.

Field Note

A flock of crows is known as a "murder of crows." Some say crows are responsible for a great many calamities that have been attributed to natural disasters. They also are capable of reading human thoughts and dictating human actions. Crows have the ability to transform from one crow to all crows and back again. Gnomes and Gnarlys are well aware of their powers and fear them above all other creatures, next to humans.

Chapter Seventeen

Calling the Crow

❧

"CROW," repeated Newt, dropping the word like a stone into the silence.

"Crow?" The Oldest Gnome, his white hair matted with pine pitch, stumbled toward Newt. His voice shook with emotion. "So now you mean to summon the crow?!! *That* is the Gnarly plan? To bring the wrath down on all of us?!"

Newt was confused. He did not have a plan at all. He simply announced what he had heard. But the very word "crow" had a way of becoming something else.

Crows are greatly feared in North Woods and in all woods. Their powers are legendary, their motives dark and mysterious. Sometimes crows do good things, sometimes bad. The problem is, you never know which.

The word had set off a new round of insults among the Gnomes and Gnarlys.

"A typical Gnarly plan," roared the Wisest, trying to extricate himself from a wad of gooble. "Heap trouble upon trouble."

"Yes," piped the Foolish Gnome, whose face and green jacket were smeared with grape stains. "We were *all* foolish to come here in the first place."

Newt hopped up and down trying to explain he had not meant anything at all, but his voice came out like a mouse squeak in a hurricane.

Netherby was uncharacteristically silent throughout the discussions. Though Newt had not meant that a crow should be summoned, Netherby realized it could be their answer to the human dilemma.

Crows can do what few other creatures are capable of. They have powers over humans. For centuries they have wreaked havoc on the human world—for reasons only they know.

"Our only hope . . . ," he began, gazing around the gruf from Gnome face to Gnarly face, then back to stare into the eyes of the smallest Gnarly, "is to call the crow."

"Me?" squeaked Newt. "But . . . surely, Netherby, . . . you have more words . . ."

"Too many," came Nodwart's voice from the recesses of the gruf. "It's you, Newt."

"It's only fitting," replied Netherby, "since your juju got us into this mess in the first place."

~⚬~

That night, an unseasonable cold settled over North Woods. A three-quarter moon rose over the tops of the trees. Newt stood just out of the moonlight, at the bottom of Highbush Hill, in a depression at the base of a boulder. It was unwise to stand in the open and call crows. Gnarlys and Gnomes knew this instinctively, without having to refer to *How Nature Works.*

The other Gnarlys and Gnomes were hidden behind a patch of ground cedar. They could not see Newt, only puffs of his breath rising up from the boulder. Every once in a while a shiver ran from Gnarly to Gnome. Every once in a while a Gnome would stare accusingly at a Gnarly and a Gnarly would scrunch his nose up at a Gnome. Otherwise, they were silent and focused on the boulder.

They shared one common thought: Each was glad not to be Newt at that moment.

After a while, they began to wonder if fear had frozen Newt's vocal cords. It had been a long time since the little Gnarly, in full uniform, had stationed himself in front of the boulder to perform his mission. Netherby and the Gnomes had given him many words to use in making his request of the crow. As for calling the crow, that was up to Newt's juju, except for one instruction from Netherby: No thrushes.

Calling crows is delicate work. To call any bird, the sound must be utterly convincing; to call a crow is harder still. It is not just a matter of duplicating the call. It is to call the spirits that call the crows. This is part of Newt's juju.

Despite the urgency of the situation and the impatience of the Gnarlys and Gnomes behind him, Newt would not rush his call. It was too important. In fact, without even knowing it, Newt had waited his whole life for just such a moment. The call had to come on its own.

The undulating *ow-wee* of a coyote rose into the still night air, answered by another coyote. The Gnomes and Gnarlys thought this was the sound that Newt had made, but shortly after the coyotes' calls had faded away, another sound rose. It made the fur stand up all over the Gnarlys' bodies and bristled the Gnomes' eyebrows.

They knew then that this sound came from Newt.

I don't think I can describe the sound exactly, though I could hear it clearly from here. It began as a quiver, as a katy-did might make in the high grasses; then it rose to the piercing squeal of a hawk and then it became something else—not insect, bird, or mammal. Something beyond North Woods and South Woods and all woods. It spun out into the night, a howling, hungry cry, stalking the stars.

When the sound left the sky, all creatures of the forest—the animals and birds and insects, Gnomes and Gnarlys—leaned after it, peering into the sky. It was a long time before silence filled back in completely.

In this silence, Gnomes and Gnarlys listened for the answer of the crow. It did not come, and it did not come. The forest was silent.

Newt had puffed himself up to try another call when the answer came. It lifted the edge of silence enough to slip in, then cracked the air like a nut. It was a murder of crows coming from all directions. A trembling mass of Gnarlys and Gnomes huddled together as they looked to the sky for a storm of crows descending.

A black streak swept across the moon and landed with a splash of wings a mere foot in front of Newt. It was one crow.

She cocked her head like a question mark and studied the terrified Gnarly. Newt had never been so close to a crow before. She was huge. Her black feathers gleamed in the moonlight. Moon filled her eyes.

Newt was shaking so hard he did not know if he could get out what he had to say. The crow spoke first.

"A Gnarly?" the crow's voice crackled on the crisp night air. "I thought the dinosaurs had returned."

Newt's nose twitched with pride. His call had been good enough to impress a crow! Then he tried to remember the words that Netherby and the Gnomes had given him to say. But before he could find them, the crow said, "You called for help."

Newt nodded. He was trying to think of the next thing he was supposed to say, but now he had lost all his words.

"It must be something very serious for a Gnarly to call a crow." There was a glint of satisfaction in the moon-white eyes. "What could it be?"

Newt opened his mouth again, but the crow, with a ruffle of feathers, answered her own question.

"Something too big for your trickery to get you out of, yes? Something you probably started yourself, yes? What could it be . . .?" Newt started to form the word, but the crow snatched it from him. "Humans. Of course." She opened her beak wide and coughed out a laugh. "The biggest trouble there is. Brought down on the naughty Gnarlys of North Woods."

The night erupted in laughter. It sounded like thousands of crows were laughing at once, compounded by echoes answering echoes.

"And Gnomes," Newt managed.

"Gnomes and Gnarlys together?" the crow cocked her head again. Her eyes sparked so brightly it made Newt blink. He couldn't keep his eyes off the crow's beak, which was long and curved with bristles sprouting around its base. Crows have been known to capture Gnarlys and drop them like seeds far away, just for the evil delight of it.

"But I see only you," continued the crow. "They must be hiding somewhere nearby watching the proceedings, their jowls atremble." She snickered. Then she turned her attention back to Newt, the tip of her beak dangerously close to the Gnarly's nose. "So, you have gotten yourself into a heap of human trouble."

Newt didn't reply. He now knew the crow had the answers to all her own questions.

"What could they want?" asked the crow, lowering her head to gaze directly into Newt's eyes. "Perhaps it was something they heard. Something that stirred up their curiosity. The human curiosity is very, very hungry, you know. Once it is awakened it must be fed or it will suck up streams, devour mountains, chomp down forests until it is satisfied."

Newt gasped in horror. "How do we stop their curiosity?"

"You can't," replied the crow. "No Gnarly juju is good enough. And there is nothing in *How Nature Works* to help either!" Newt opened his mouth to ask the next question, but the crow answered before he could get it out. "You must feed it . . . something."

Newt was sure that something would be a Gnarly, and worse, that Gnarly would be him.

Once again, the crow read the Gnarly's mind.

"Not a Gnarly. They would poke and prod you and put you in a jar." The crow stretched out her neck to be eye to eye with Newt. "Or . . ." she continued, "there's another option. The neck snapped back, turtle-like, between her shoulders. "You can starve it!" The crow bobbed her head in excitement. "Yes, yes, I know just what you need for this job, Gnarly." The crow looked absolutely delighted with herself. "Something phantasmagorical!"

Newt would have asked what that meant, but the crow concluded the interview. The bird lifted her wings and, in one flap, disappeared into the night with a clamorous *caw, caw, caw.*

It sounded like a murder of crows.

When the last *caw* had dwindled from the sky, Newt hurried back up the hill. The others came out of hiding and gathered around him, each asking the same question over the other: *What did the crow say?*

Newt tried to remember what the crow had said, but mostly he recalled sucked up streams and chomped down forests. When he tried to repeat the big word the crow used at the end, all he could get out was the first syllable.

This was very frustrating to Netherby, who was sure the word Newt could not remember was the thing that would drive the humans out of the woods.

"Phantoms? Fangs? Fascists?" Netherby prodded.

Newt shook his head wearily. He was exhausted from his encounter with the crow and knew he would not sleep without seeing those moon-bright eyes and sharp, carrying-away beak pointed at him.

"More important than how the crows will drive the humans out of the woods," said the Foolish Gnome, "is what they will demand in return."

Field Note

Gnarlys and Gnomes use a network of "runs" between and under vegetation. If you part tall grasses and ferns and look closely into tufts of feather moss and club moss you may find the faint trace of a Gnome or Gnarly run winding through them. Don't expect to find tracks. They are too faint to see with the naked eye.

Chapter Eighteen

The Mushroom Feast

❧

GNARLYS and Gnomes were eight smudges on the moonlit forest floor as they trudged up the hill toward Sweet Fat Mama.

Nothing was said about why the Gnomes did not return to their own den or one of their Just-in-Case burrows. Humans and their dragons had rearranged the forest and wiped out many of the familiar traces and landmarks. The Gnomes would not be able to successfully navigate the forest for days. Besides, Gnomes and Gnarlys were consumed with two burning questions: How the crows would rid the forest of humans and what they would demand in return.

"You can't trust crows," said the Oldest Gnome, once they had entered the gruf. "Only a Gnarly would come up with such a scheme!"

"That puny Gnarly over there with the exploding head!" roared the Wisest, pointing toward Newt. Newt opened his mouth to defend himself but knew it was of no use. He slumped in the corner of the gruf instead, wiggled out of his uniform and pulled off his helmet.

The angle of the moon cast just the faintest light into the gruf.

"What's for dinner?" asked a Nubbin from the darkness.

"Sometimes I think Nubbins are no more than presentable Gnarlys," grumbled the Oldest. "All they think about are their own comforts."

"Food is not a comfort. Food is a necessity!" piped the hungry Nubbin, who instantly regretted talking back to the elder Gnome and sank out of sight into the furthest corner of Sweet Fat Mama.

"Let's eat then," said Netherby with a shrug, as if it was just a matter of saying it.

But a quick glance around Sweet Fat Mama yielded only the chaos they had left behind: disassembled traps and catapults, broken acorn caps, shreds of cattail fluff stuck in gooble, crushed galls, smashed berries, and an upside-down beetle with its legs churning in the air.

The Gnarlys seemed quite at home in the wreckage, but the Gnomes looked glum. In their own snug den, the Gnomes would feast on ample stores of woodland harvests laid up for the long winter months ahead.

Gnarlys, on the other hand, live season to season, day to day. When they get hungry, they simply follow one of their tunnels out to the forest to see what the season has to offer—nuts and berries, or perhaps a tasty nightcrawler to give them a wrestle. And, of course, in the winter, they can raid the Gnomes' supplies when the Gnomes venture out of their den to investigate how Nature is getting along without them.

Now, with humans prowling the woods the Gnarlys had fewer choices.

"We'll just tap on Sweet Fat Mama," said Netherby.

"Shows how much you Gnarlys know," the Oldest snorted. "Maples don't give sap in the fall. They are preparing for winter—something you Gnarlys should have thought of."

"Besides, Netherby, Sweet Fat Mama doesn't give us sap even in the right season," said Newt. Netherby scowled at Newt. An out of sight Nubbin made a noise that might have been a cough, or perhaps it was a chuckle.

"Earthworms," suggested Nodwart.

"Earthworms?" said the Oldest with disgust. "Gnomes are strictly vegetarian."

"Strictly vegetarian," Netherby mimicked.

There was an exchange of angry looks, interrupted by Nodwart's "aha." Nodwart had an idea.

Not one to explain his ideas, which came around every sixth moon or so, Nodwart grabbed his rucklesack and scurried about until he found one of the escape tunnels that hadn't been crushed by humans. In his tiny mind was the picture of some fall mushrooms just breaking ground downhill of Sweet Fat Mama. There would be more than enough mushrooms to feed all the Gnarlys and the persnickety Gnomes.

Out the tunnel and into the moonlight, Nodwart quickly became confused. The humans had left a different landscape of bent and broken bushes, uprooted saplings and rutted earth. He could not locate the run to the place where the mushrooms grew, and so he started back to the gruf. That's when he found the mushrooms.

They may have been the same mushrooms he saw the day before or they may have been different mushrooms, but they looked close enough, growing all by themselves full in the moonlight under a white pine. Two had been crushed, but one fine specimen remained. It was a tall orange mushroom with pale, petal-like flecks over the cap.

Keeping a sharp eye out for owls, Nodwart shimmied up the stem to the broad, umbrella top where he set to work tearing pieces from the choicest part of the cap and stuffing them into his rucklesack. Then, he slid down the mushroom stem and, quite by luck, found himself before one of the intact tunnels leading into Sweet Fat Mama. Breathless with excitement and very proud of himself, Nodwart deposited his harvest in the middle of the gruf for all to admire and feast upon.

The Gnomes' faces crinkled up as they examined the bits of mushroom. The Foolish Gnome kicked a piece with the toe of his pointy boot. "You can't eat just any mushroom," he said. "Even a Nubbin knows that."

"These aren't just any mushrooms," said Netherby, choosing a plump piece of the cap. "They are Gloriflorias. We eat them all the time. In fact, we cultivate them."

"Cultivate? Harrumph. When did a Gnarly ever cultivate anything?" grumbled the Foolish Gnome. If the Gnomes had brought *How Nature Works,* he would leaf through it to see if such a species as Glorifloria existed.

"You are welcome to go hungry, Gnomes," said Netherby, popping the Gloriforia into his mouth.

The Gnarlys set to eating, hunching over the mushroom pieces with great delight, making contented lip-smacking noises, while the Gnomes looked on with disdain.

Only later that evening, when the Gnarlys were snoring their snorts and whistles, wren song, and bullfrog croak, did one of the Nubbins creep over to the pieces of mushroom littering the floor of Sweet Fat Mama. The Nubbin took one cautious bite, then another. Then he reached for another piece. The other Nubbin joined in and soon they were making the same lip-smacking noises the Gnarlys had made.

The Oldest and Wisest and Foolish Gnomes crossed their arms over their empty bellies and watched the Nubbins with disapproval.

Once the Nubbins had fallen contentedly asleep, the three Gnomes stared hungrily at the scattered morsels of mushrooms that remained. Finally, unable to resist any longer, the Wisest, whose big empty belly was beginning to roar like a lion was trapped inside, snatched up a piece of mushroom and gobbled it down without a word.

Then the Oldest did the same. Finally, the Foolish Gnome did, too.

Field Note

⸻

While Gnomes are strictly vegetarian, Gnarlys will eat anything from mushrooms to earthworms. They often retrieve bits of food left by humans along the trail. They are especially fond of chewing gum (gooble) and the white stuff inside Oreo cookies.

⸻

Chapter Nineteen

Glorafloria Dreams

❧

UNLIKE humans and many animals, when Gnomes and Gnarlys fall asleep, they seldom dream. So, when the mushrooms they had eaten brought on vivid dreams, they seemed not to be dreams at all, but horribly, horribly real events.

The Gnomes shared the same dream. It went like this: Each awoke to stare into a crow's eye sockets, which held no eyes at all, just endless black space that could be fallen into.

"Shh, don't wake the others," said the crow in a secretive voice. I will show you where to go to escape the humans. Then you will show the others."

"Where is it?" asked the Gnome.

"A safe place," came the reply.

"Is it far from North Woods?" asked the Gnome.

"No, no. It is just in case the worst happens. Just over the hill. Just in case . . ."

Gnomes like to have a just-in-case, so the Gnome nodded and climbed on the back of the crow. Just as he did, there was a terrible sound like the earth had cracked open and the crow carried the Gnome out of this world and into endless space.

In the Gnarly dream, each Gnarly awakened to find himself alone in an unfamiliar place. All of the trees and bushes and even the stream were gone and there was nothing to remind him of North Woods. There were no birds or animals and not a single Gnarly. Not even a Gnome. The Gnarly traveled alone through the strange, barren landscape until at last, he saw something as familiar as another Gnarly—Sweet Fat Mama on the crest of the hill, looking the same as always, except that nothing grew around her.

The Gnarly ran as fast as he could toward the giant tree and just as he got close enough to see the entrance, the leaves and branches and bark fell to the ground, leaving only an empty shell. With nothing to shelter him from predators, the Gnarly ran and ran. A crow screamed above him, then circled, savoring the Gnarly's desperation, waiting for just the right moment to strike and carry him into endless space.

Then both the Gnome and Gnarly dreams broke apart into many random terrors. There were snarling coyotes and giant holes, gouged out forests, swirling blackness and terrible sounds and colors throbbing in their heads, desperate to get out.

Gnomes and Gnarlys awoke at the same time and looked around Sweet Fat Mama in dazed silence. It was completely dark outside, though it seemed it should be morning. There was a look of panic on each Gnome and Gnarly face. No one knew what to say.

A Nubbin spoke first. In a small, nervous voice he asked, "It *was* a dream, wasn't it?"

"Of course," whispered the Wisest after some time.

"But what did the terrible things in the dream mean?"

"They meant," snorted the Foolish Gnome from the other end of the gruf, "never trust a Gnarly's choice of mushrooms!"

Field Note

There is no such mushroom as a Glorifloria. The mushroom the Gnarlys and Gnomes ate was an Amanita muscaria, a tasty but mind-bending mushroom. The Gnarlys know little about mushrooms and eat them indiscriminately, having avoided the most poisonous by sheer luck. The Gnomes are usually very careful about the mushrooms they eat, consulting How Nature Works *for spore prints and precise descriptions before sampling.*

Chapter Twenty

When SsaA Comes

❧

WHILE the Gnomes and Gnarlys were still deep inside their Glorafloria dreams, the crow was summoning her powers to deal with the human invasion of North and South Woods.

Crows, you see, have contact with worlds beyond this one and can call upon any number of agents to perform their magic. The crow that Newt had called chose the most powerful of spirits. Surely this was not necessary for the task at hand, but crows love devilment as much as Gnarlys do, only crow devilment is much bigger.

It happened on a sparkling fall day, two days after Newt had called the crow.

❧

I had just returned to my gruf after a full day of tracking Gnarlys. Though it was a calm night, with a full moon rising, there was something unsettled about the air. I tried to go through my notes but couldn't get comfortable.

The air was rapidly growing colder. I put away my notes and hurried outside to find more wood for the night, hoping to drive out that awful chill and sense of uneasiness.

The moon lit the forest floor like a stage, and I had no trouble finding wood for the fire. With my arms full, I started back toward the good oak. Then everything went black. Black as a crow's heart. I had to feel my way to the entrance.

By the time I did, the air had turned to ice. I couldn't see anything, but I know every inch of the inside of this oak and knew just where the hearth was and where I keep the matches. I quickly laid the fire and struck the match. My hands were shaking plenty, so I wasn't surprised that it didn't light the first time. But the puzzling thing was, there wasn't even a spark. I struck the match again. Nothing. Again. Nothing.

Then the sound.

It was like . . . like . . . you know when you suck in a big breath just before you blow out all the candles on a birthday cake? This was like that, only big enough to suck all the oxygen out of the forest. I expected it would blow a wind so terrible it would topple every tree in the forest. I crept to the entrance of the oak, looked out.

Then it came. No, not a wind. There was no wind at all. Just a slithery, fur-raising sound.

SsaA it hissed. SsaA.

And I knew.

No one can say what SsaA is, where it comes from or where it goes. All I know is that it is not of this earth.

I could not imagine what had summoned such a powerful spirit. I knew that humans had nothing to do with it. Gnomes and Gnarlys exaggerate the humans' powers. They think humans are far beyond their understanding, but humans are not that complicated.

∽❦∾

With Gnomes and Gnarlys deep in slumber, SsaA stalked North and South Woods, extinguishing all light and earthly warmth.

SsaA, it sighed. *SsaA*. Like the last gasp of all the earth's lost and forgotten souls.

When it finally faded away, I held my breath, then prayed it would not return. But something more terrifying filled the silence left by its passing. The beat of wings on air, the thrash of leaves and crack of limbs as every bird and animal fled the forest.

SsaA drove everything that could slither, crawl, fly, run, or waddle out of the forest. Then all was still. The moon reappeared.

I crept outside. There was no damage done to the oak. Not a single leaf or branch was taken. The forest was just as it had been.

Except for the silence.

Field Note

—

The humans who invaded North and South Woods were not intent on destruction. They were desperate to know what made the strange call that came from Newt. Humans' hunger to know what a thing is, to fasten a name to it, can be destructive, even if they don't mean it to be.

—

Chapter Twenty-One

What Is All the Silence About?

～⊛～

THE rising sun peeked into the Gnarly gruf.

The Wisest climbed out of sleep first, amid Gnarly snores of snorts and croaks and whistles and Gnome snores of jumbly grumbles. He was dismayed to see by the angle of the sun through the entrance of the gruf that it was far past early morning. He did not realize it was far past early morning of three days later.

The gruf was in a terrible mess of shreds of this, scraps of that, and tossed and tumbled bodies. It was hard to tell a Gnome from a Gnarly.

The Wisest stumbled over to the scraps of mushroom scattered about the floor of the gruf. "Gloraflorias," he muttered in disgust as he stomped each piece into the dirt until they were just dark smudges.

The Wisest had a throbbing headache from all the bad mushroom dreams and he was in a foul mood. He snatched his cap from under the out-flung arm of a Nubbin, then gazed with contempt upon the open mouths and unseemly sprawl of Gnarlys, Gnomes, and Nubbins.

With a loud *harrumph*, he stepped over the Oldest Gnome who was snoring especially loudly and picked his way to the entrance of the gruf. He rubbed his eyes and peered out into the forest.

There was evidence of humans everywhere—crushed and uprooted bushes, tire tracks gouged into the earth, scraped bark, severed limbs. But there were no humans anywhere to be seen.

Had calling the crow worked? Had the crow devised some magic to chase the humans away, or had the humans simply gotten bored with this little pocket of woods and gone back to the Way-Way Yonda?

The Wisest shook his head. He did not want to put another puzzle into it. He stepped outside. The sunlight struck him like an accusation, and he staggered back against the tree. But, gradually, the warmth made him feel better, and he scratched his head and patted down his bristly beard. He sniffed the air. There was so much work to be gotten to.

Many of the Gnomes' Just-in-Case holes needed to be stocked; they had to remind the ever-procrastinating cedar waxwings to stop their berry gorging and prepare for their migration south; they had to get the woolly bears tucked away and prod the toads to bury themselves in mud, and the wood frogs and salamanders to find their woodland burrows.

He had not yet noticed that there was not a single bird, animal, insect, or amphibian to be found anywhere in the forest.

The Wisest's ambitions were stalled by a troubling thought. What if the humans came back? If they did, all work would have to be put aside again for days, or perhaps for weeks. "We had nothing to do with this predicament," he grumbled, looking longingly into the forest. "This is truly a Gnarly mess we are stuck in the middle of."

Though the Wisest was speaking to no one in particular, one of the Nubbins had awakened and followed him outside the tree and said with great seriousness as if he were the Wisest himself, "It smells like a Gnarly trick to me." This was a Nubbin with ambitions of taking over the role of the Wisest Gnome someday.

The Wisest gave the Nubbin a dismissive *harrumph*, turned his back on him, and folded his arms across his chest. The Nubbin hopped around to face the Wisest. "It *is* a Gnarly trick," he repeated, now becoming excited with his revelation. "The false winter, the mushrooms, humans in our woods. It's all Gnarly juju. They can make you hear a bird that isn't. They can make you think it's winter when it isn't. They can make you see what never was."

The Wisest stared past him.

"Don't you see?" insisted the Nubbin, who had not yet realized that he had gone too far. The Wisest had had enough of this Nubbin's impertinence. He swiped him aside, sending the Nubbin tumbling down the hill into a clump of partridgeberry. Then the Gnome settled down on an exposed rootlet to ponder the puzzlement of recent events.

Just a Gnarly trick? Was all of this—the humans, the crows—just a part of Gnarly juju? The three were inside, nestled in thistledown, snoring as if they hadn't a concern in the world.

Before long, he heard a rustling behind him. The Wisest turned to see the Foolish Gnome striding a little uncertainly in his direction, using his whittlestick for support.

"Don't trouble yourself," said the Wisest out of the side of his mouth. "The morning started without you."

Either the Foolish Gnome did not hear or pretended not to. He was looking around the forest, gazing from tree to tree, bush to bush, up into the sky.

"This foolishness with humans and crows is all the work of Gnarlys!" announced the Wisest. "I don't suppose you thought of that," he added, glancing over at the Foolish Gnome.

Of course, the Nubbin, who was now indignantly spitting out partridgeberry seeds, had thought of that, but Nubbins, no matter what their ambitions, do not count yet as Gnomes and any small insight they might have is dismissed or claimed by a Gnome.

The notion that it had all been a Gnarly trick—the humans, the crows, the mushroom dream—became a certainty as the Gnomes all gathered outside Sweet Fat Mama. The bright fall day reassured them that nothing was wrong in the world—except that Gnarlys were still in it.

Hoisting their whittlesticks high in the air, the Gnomes advanced down the hill, set on getting back to work immediately, all the while peering around for humans, just in case. They were not as sure as they appeared that it had all been a Gnarly trick. After all, they had seen the humans and the crow for themselves but wrapping it all up as a Gnarly trick was much less to think about. The Gnomes just wanted to get back to business.

◦◦◦

"Whew," exclaimed a Nubbin nervously after a while, "not a human . . . in sight."

It was true. Not a human anywhere. But the Gnomes began to feel uneasy. For the first time, it occurred to them that something was wrong. Very wrong. North Woods did not seem like North Woods.

It wasn't something there so much as something *not* there. The sunlight that poured through the leaves of the maples and beech and birch did not bounce off any wings. The small breeze that lifted the leaves did not ruffle any fur. No bright eyes or bushy tail flashed out of the cavity of trees or darted through shadows. The woods were silent. Absolutely silent. Then, even the breeze died down as if it was the last gasp of life in the forest.

The first thing the Gnomes thought was that they had slept through a terrible storm. After a violent storm, the creatures of the forest, even the wind, are still. But this was more than stillness. This was gone. Everything gone.

On a beautiful early October day when squirrels and chipmunks would be dashing back and forth across the forest floor, chattering incessantly as they stored up acorns for the winter; when bees would be visiting the thistles, goldenrod, and asters collecting their last stores of nectar and pollen; when cicadas would be serenading the season and birds would be feeding and jabbering, gathering their families for the long journey south, there was only silence.

The silence reached deep inside Sweet Fat Mama where it roused Netherby from a deep slumber. He also knew something was wrong, though he didn't know just what. He shook Newt and Nodwart, who awoke snorting and spitting. Shushing them silent, Netherby tiptoed up to the entrance of the gruf.

He spied the Gnomes halfway down the slope. They seemed to be studying the forest. He watched as they advanced down the hill a little farther, then froze, as if they had been caught in a sudden arctic wind. They took another few, tentative steps, disappearing from view except for the peaks of their bright red caps.

"I wonder what those Gnomes are up to now," said Netherby.

The Gnarlys followed the Gnomes cautiously, straining to catch a word or two. Suddenly, Newt straightened up as if something had just occurred to him. "What is all the silence about?" he blurted.

The Foolish Gnome swung around first, then all the Gnome faces were aimed at the Gnarlys. They looked like burning coals inside tufts of beard.

"Aha," snarled the Foolish Gnome. "The sleeping beauties have awakened." The Gnarlys looked from one to the other. "What trick is this, Gnarlys?" The Foolish Gnome waved his whittlestick in the air.

The Gnarlys stood pressed close together in one big knot of furriness.

"There is nothing left in the forest," accused the Wisest Gnome. "Or is this just another mushroom dream?" The Wisest sounded more bewildered than angry.

Before the Gnarlys could answer, or before the Gnomes could accuse them of anything more, Netherby spied something on the horizon. He pointed and everyone turned to see.

"That thrush is not a dream," he said haughtily, but with great relief at the same time.

It was hardly more than a speck on the blue sky. Gnomes and Gnarlys watched as the bird came closer and closer. It was not a thrush, corrected the Wisest Gnome, but a blue jay; it was not a blue jay, claimed the Foolish Gnome, but a robin; it was not a robin, insisted the Oldest, but a hawk.

Newt, who had known from the very first dab on the horizon what the bird was, said nothing.

Field Note

As young apprentice Gnomes, Nubbins have little say in Gnome affairs. They do not have beards and dress in shifts made from squirrel fur that is not dyed the lustrous reds and greens of the Gnomes' wear.

— *Chapter Twenty-Two* —

Phantasmagoria

❧

THE crow shone metallic blue in the sun as it bobbed on a branch of a sapling. She cocked her head from side to side, eyeing the terrified bundle of Gnomes, Gnarlys, and Nubbins just a few feet away.

"Are the humans gone?" dared the Wisest.

The crow did not answer immediately. When she did, her voice was full of venomous glee.

"Don't tell me . . . you missed it?! Sound asleep in your mushroom dreams?!" The crow's voice gonged like a bell in the silence. "When SsaA comes, nothing stays. Only silence. And humans hate silence."

At the word "SsaA," Gnomes and Gnarlys looked at one another in astonishment.

The Gnomes had heard of SsaA in lore but did not believe in it. It was not even mentioned in *How Nature Works*. The Gnarlys knew nothing whatsoever about SsaA except that they did not like the way the name made them feel, like it was crawling up their backs.

"But . . . what . . . is . . . SsaA?" stuttered a Nubbin before the Wisest gave him a sharp jab. "And how . . .?" The Wisest slapped his hand over the Nubbin's mouth. It was bad luck to ask a crow "how" they did anything. It was a habit of crows to demonstrate just "how" on whoever asked.

"All" . . . Nodwart gasped . . . "gone." His voice sounded lonely in the creatureless forest.

Then the crow began to laugh, and it became all crows laughing, an avalanche of noise into the silence. Gnomes and Gnarlys crouched as if the sky might fall around them.

"You should be careful what you ask for, Gnarly. You summoned the crow. The crow summoned SsaA," said many crows at once.

The truth of this hit the Gnomes and Gnarlys at once. By calling the crow they had unleashed a terrible curse upon the forest, worse than any human invasion.

"We want it back," ventured Newt nervously. "All the buzz and *whirp* and *cheep* and *pratter*."

Gnomes and Gnarlys glanced around the forest as if they might find a buzz and *whirp* within a clump of yew, or a *cheep* and *pratter* in the leaves of the maple. A forest without these sounds was unimaginable. The forest would die without all the animals and insects that made these sounds.

"Use your juju, Gnarlys," came the crow's impatient reply. "You are clever enough to stir up human curiosity; clever enough to call the crow. Now, are you clever enough to call Nature back?"

Netherby opened his mouth to speak, but the crow had spread her wings and lifted off from the branch. For an instant, the sky turned black with crows, then the mass dissolved into a single crow, a pinprick in the bright blue sky. Gnomes and Gnarlys watched until it had completely disappeared. Then they turned to look accusingly at one another.

"That's what you get when you consort with crows!" said Netherby to Newt.

"That's what you get when you make mischief with humans," shot back the Wisest to Netherby.

Then Gnomes and Gnarlys slumped in despair. Without the noise of their own squabbling, the silence of the forest poured down on them. So, they began to pick fights with one another again, just to keep from drowning in silence, until they wore themselves out.

"I didn't know silence could be so big," said Netherby. Suddenly, he felt totally exhausted.

Not knowing what to do about such a terrible calamity, the Gnarlys retreated to Sweet Fat Mama and fluffed up the scattered pieces of thistledown, cattail fluff and moss to prepare for a little snooze. The silence, the anger of the Gnomes, the terror of the crow, and the hard thinking about it all had tired them out before the day had begun. Gnarlys, as you probably know by now, do not think about a subject any longer than it takes to get hungry or dozy.

They were just about to tumble back into sleep when a Gnome shadow appeared at the sunlit entrance of the gruf. Netherby was the only Gnarly with one eye still open, and he watched the shadow become the form of the Oldest Gnome, grunting and wobbling in the direction of the Gnarlys. The Oldest had not spoken for a long time, but now it appeared, when his wheezing and snorting stopped, he was about to. Netherby closed his eye and pretended to be asleep.

"Sleep?" The Oldest Gnome's voice had gone darkly sweet like overripe blackberries. "On no, Gnarly, you will not sleep."

The sweetness ruptured into bitterness. "Not for a long time!" The angry words spit down on the Gnarlys as they tried to wiggle deeper into the thistledown. But the Oldest was not to be ignored.

"Didn't you hear what the crow said?" he roared as he bent over the Gnarlys, his fists clenched as if he meant to pummel them all.

Clearly, no sleep was to be had. The Gnarlys opened their eyes and peered out of their bedding at the bulbous nose of the Gnome looming over them as if they had not a whiff of what he was so upset about.

"Use your juju!"

The other Gnomes, who had lingered in the background, snapped to attention at the word "juju." They quickly gathered around the Oldest and stared at him in bewilderment.

"Juju?" exclaimed the Wisest. "Now, on top of humans, crows, mushroom dreams, we pile Gnarly juju?" There was a general grumbling among the Gnomes.

Calling upon Gnarly juju was the last thing a Gnome would do. It was certainly not included in *How Nature Works*, which by the way, was back at the main Gnome den with the Voped curled up on the last chapter it had been opened to before the false winter episode: "Hibernation Habits of Woodland Creatures and What Gnomes Should Do to Keep Them on Task."

"Gnarly juju got us into this; Gnarly juju must get us out," was all the Oldest said, then waited for understanding to seep into each Gnome brain, which it eventually did.

"Aha," said the Wisest, whose brain it had seeped into last. He nodded gravely.

Dimly, the Gnarlys were beginning to understand, too.

"You Gnarlys," rumbled the Oldest, "have made mischief for centuries using your juju. You can call any bird, animal, insect. You are devilishly good at it, right?"

Newt, who was proudest of this skill, could not help himself. He sat up and nodded enthusiastically.

"Then get to work!" roared the Oldest.

The other Gnomes, now fully understanding what the Oldest had in mind, lifted their whittlesticks and bellowed the peculiar Gnome war chant: "*BAH, BAH, GRAMFUNKLE RAH.*" They stared with bright, shining eyes down on the Gnarlys.

"You brought this upon us," said the Oldest. "Now *you* fix it. Call every single bird and animal and insect back to our forest."

"The wind, too," piped a Nubbin.

"And it better be good!" added the Foolish Gnome. "Good enough so not a bird, not a mole, not a mosquito suspects for one instant that it's just another Gnarly trick."

The Gnarlys were speechless.

Sitting there on a wispy pile of thistledown, with angry Gnomes all around them, the Gnarlys realized that they had been trapped by their own tricks.

They had a lot of work to do.

Field Note

———

The forest is never silent. Next time you are in the woods on an autumn day, listen carefully to all the sounds that surround you. Then you will know how big a task the Gnarlys had ahead of them.

———

—— *Chapter Twenty-Three* ——

The Time of the Big Silence

❧

IT seemed the Gnarlys would never get another long
afternoon stretched out in the sun in front of Sweet
Fat Mama. It seemed they would never be allowed to
sleep all day on their thistledown or spend a lusciously lazy day
watching the bustle of other creatures getting ready for winter.

All talk of expeditions had ended. No more long hours por-
ing over the collection of found objects and devising catapults,
snares, and baffles for marauding Gnomes and other invaders.

Gone were all opportunities to frustrate birds, tease woodchucks, bother bees, or steal honey and pollen cakes from the
Gnomes. For one thing, there were no birds, woodchucks, or
bees to be found in the forest. But there were Gnomes everywhere, or so it seemed. The Gnarlys could not move without
Gnomes casting their shadows over them, or rest without feeling the point of a whittlestick.

It was no fun to be a Gnarly anymore. Everything had gone
Gnome-serious.

⤙☙⤚

Each morning, the Gnomes arrived at the Gnarly gruf and rustled them out of sleep.

"Okay, Gnarlys, off to the forest you go!" would boom the Foolish or Wisest or Oldest Gnome with the Nubbins chuckling and snickering behind them. No matter how quickly the Gnarlys moved, the Gnomes never thought it was quick enough, and made sure to add a jab with their whittlesticks.

The Gnarlys, grumbling and snuffling, would gather up their rucklesacks and file out into the forest.

There they met only silence. Unmovable silence. The Gnarly calls only bounced off its surface or traveled a short distance before becoming part of the silence, too.

Silence had infested North Woods.

Still, the Gnarlys tried.

They shimmied up trees and trilled, burrowed into dens and yipped, climbed hills and ululated, crossed streams and cooed. They beseeched the moon, begged the rain. They called to raccoons, squirrels, moles, mice, rabbits, chipmunks, porcupines. They appealed to turtles and frogs and even the fish in Alder Creek. They howled to the wind, again and again.

Only silence answered.

In the wee hours of night, the Gnarlys would stumble back to their gruf, only to be tumbled out of sleep by the Gnomes before the sun was up. Then, they would grumble, scratch, sniff, cough, and begin again. All day they roamed the eerily silent woods, calling and calling, their voices reaching as far as they could go.

You're probably wondering, as I wondered, why the Gnarlys did not set up their booby traps and pine pitch spills and various other clever devices for keeping the Gnomes out of Sweet Fat Mama. Or why they did not simply flee down one of their tunnels and out into the forest to hide from the Gnomes for as long as it took for them to give up the chase and go back to their Gnome business.

The answer is: This was not like any other time. This was the Time of the Big Silence. The worst time in North Woods' history.

⁓ⱺᴄ

Do you know what silence is?

You probably think you do, but there is little silence in the world you live in. There is always a whir or a buzz or a hum somewhere. Total silence is as rare as Gnarlys.

The humans who invaded North and South Woods did not return to the forest. No matter what they thought they might find there, they could not bear the weight of absolute silence. It was like space without any stars. It was like a bottomless ocean. It was like night without morning.

I can tell you those weeks living in the silent forest were the loneliest and longest weeks of my life. It almost drove me out entirely. But I held fast to my faith that Nature always comes back. I kept hoping.

The Gnomes and Gnarlys did, too. That's why the Gnarlys tried again and again to call Nature back to North Woods, with the help of the Gnomes, of course.

Each time the Gnarlys complained, each time they tried to sneak a nap or steal a snack, the hot, angry breath of Gnomes blasted orders over their shoulders, or Gnomes prodded their backsides with whittlesticks.

The Gnomes were determined that the Gnarlys would call each and every creature back, right down to the midges.

No, these were not the same lazy, mischief-making Gnarlys. They were so bedraggled at the end of each day they could hardly lift their heads or utter a sound. Their lances dragged behind them. They trailed bits of beetle wing uniforms and helmet husks. They did not hop or scamper or dance.

They withered in the silence as the forest did. Each day, the sun left the sky earlier, and each day the silence grew.

‿◎◠

One morning during the second week of the Big Silence, the Gnarlys plopped down in a pile of golden maple leaves on the shores of the silent Alder Creek. "Nature has moved out of North Woods," said Newt with a heavy sigh, "for good."

The Gnarlys were hot, tired, discouraged. Hours and hours of calling had, again, failed to bring a single tweep or *urp* or croak in reply.

Newt did most of the calling because he was the most skillful, but without the songs of Nature to draw from, his voice had begun to betray him. When he croaked, he irked; when he warbled, he wobbled, when he hooted, he coughed. He feared he had lost his juju.

The Gnomes, who seemed to be always casting their angry shadows over the Gnarlys, were at that moment lolling nearby on a shelf mushroom at the base of a birch stump. The silence had infected them, too. Their anger had started to seep away and they seemed simply grumbly most of the time.

"Maybe it's time for Gnarlys to move, too," said Netherby in a low voice.

Of the Gnarlys, Netherby was the most affected by the silence. He did not curl up like a caterpillar, the usual Gnarly response to extreme stress, but he was not the same Netherby, either.

He no longer bothered to wear his uniform. He seemed naked without it. His luxuriant chestnut fur was thin and matted. Pink hide could be seen through the fur on his shoulders. Netherby had not begun to grow his winter coat of gray and brown. He would not survive the winter without it.

"Where Gnarlys go?" asked Nodwart. Nodwart had at least started to grow his white winter coat. He sat opposite Netherby looking almost as glum. He was thinking of his view of the Way-Way Yonda from high atop the red maple. Then, he had not been able to see Sweet Fat Mama in all the largeness. A Gnarly could get lost forever there.

Netherby shuddered. He was remembering the mushroom dream about the skeletal forest.

"Maybe it's like this in South Woods, too, and the Way-Way Yonda," he said, with a vacant look in his eyes. Maybe SsaA," and he shuddered when he said the name, "started an epidemic of silence. Maybe Nature is too far gone to call back."

◦⟲◦

Just past noon, long before their day was due to end, Netherby and Nodwart dragged their tired bodies back to Sweet Fat Mama. The Gnomes, just as tired and discouraged, did not have the ambition to chase the Gnarlys back to work. They trudged off down the hill to their own den, trailing their whittlesticks behind them.

Newt did not follow the others.

He squatted in a carpet of leaves by Alder Creek, Netherby's words heavy on his mind. Could it be that . . . thing . . . had chased Nature out of North Woods for good? Would his juju ever be able to reach far enough to call Nature back? He hugged himself, chilled by the thought.

Since the beginning of the Time of the Big Silence, Newt had been visited by a recurring dream. Perhaps it was brought upon by the lingering effects of the Gloraflorias, except that this was not a terrifying dream and it was not shared by the other Gnarlys.

It was always the same: The song of the wood thrush, rising up out of the silence, then falling to the earth like rain. Where each note fell, another song grew.

The dream was so real the song still played in his head after he awoke. He was sure he could make the song exactly as it was in his dream if he had not used up the last of his juju. He remembered the summer evening he and the thrush were locked in an asking and answering song, and how the bird had come to him.

If he asked now, would the wood thrush answer?

He got to his feet and walked into a clearing between trees where the last rays of the sun pooled on the forest floor. He was in clear view of predators, but he knew he would not be harmed. All the predators were gone. There was nothing to fear but failure.

Newt threw back his head, closed his eyes. He pulled the wood thrush song from his dream into his chest, up his throat, then released it on air. But the sound he made was not a song.

It was a sob.

Inside Sweet Fat Mama, Netherby and Nodwart stood looking around as if seeing their gruf for the first time. They were afraid that soon they would see it for the last time.

Sick in spirit, they chewed disconsolately on some dried acorn pieces, tossed them aside after only a few bites, and flopped back against the wall of the tree in exhaustion.

They had a hard time drifting off to sleep in the stone silence of the gruf. When sleep did come, it was quickly disturbed.

Something had flown into the house of silence. They opened their eyes. It was a sound that seemed to come from a very long time ago.

"Oh," yawned Netherby, "Newt must be practicing his juju." They tried to fall back into sleep, but this time they were awakened by the patter of running feet coming toward them.

"Don't those Gnomes ever sleep?!" grumbled Netherby.

But it was not the Gnomes. It was Newt. He stood in the entrance to the gruf, a tiny gray figure, out of breath and hopping with excitement.

The first three notes of a thrushes' song drifted into the gruf behind him. The two stared at Newt.

"It's a thrush! A wood thrush!" Newt shouted as loud as his broken voice would allow. "Nature's back!"

Field Note

—

The Time of the Big Silence is not mentioned in any field guide, but if you happen to find a copy of How Nature Works *just lying around somewhere (you won't, of course), or if you make the acquaintance of a friendly Gnome who will lend you a copy (not likely, either), you will find quite a lengthy chapter detailing the episode.*

—

Chapter Twenty-Four

Wheeps and Urps, Razzes and Eeks

⊸⊶

THE Gnarlys clamored out of Sweet Fat Mama and peered into the sunlit forest. Soon, the song rose again. Still, it was just the beginning notes, as if the bird was a little nervous to go up against such awesome silence.

Everything in Newt wanted to answer the call, but he dared not. He could no longer trust his juju.

All the Gnarlys could do was wait and listen. Then the notes came again, rising, rising, and this time, they did not fall short but spilled into a waterfall of sound. The Gnarlys, keeping as silent as they could, hopped up and down excitedly as the song came once again, daring to reach farther and farther into the forest.

As the Gnarlys bathed in the music, they detected the wobbly form of Gnomes coming up Highbush Hill toward Sweet Fat Mama. The Gnarlys could hear the little puffs of Gnome breath on the chill air as they approached, but, for once, the Gnomes said nothing. They listened, too.

They could have said that it was the wrong time of year for a wood thrush to be singing, that it should have migrated by now to South America where it spent the winters. They could have said this because it was all in *How Nature Works*, but for once, the Gnomes did not say a word.

Just as it was in Newt's dream, as each note touched the ground, another note grew. More and more songs filled North Woods.

The trill of the dark-eyed junco, the *wheep* of the tufted titmouse, the chickadee's *chicka-dee-dee-dee,* and the scold of the jay.

It was magic. It was Nature.

Gnomes and Gnarlys stood under the wide branches of Sweet Fat Mama and listened as if the songs were honeysuckle dew after a winter of starvation. It had been so long since they had heard anything except their own arguing voices.

Songs and calls piled on top of and between one another and underneath, too. Wail of the coyote and yip of foxes, the scurry and scolding of squirrels, the shriek of chipmunks, the mews and gurgles and caws.

By the time morning washed over the woods, songs had filled in the silence so completely it seemed there couldn't be another one wedged in.

"Well," said Netherby, straightening himself to his full height. He smoothed back the thinning fur behind his ears. He looked very much like he was going to say something like *I guess we showed you, Gnomes,* but thought better of it. "Well," he repeated and quickly sat down.

"Well . . . what?" asked the Oldest Gnome, striding over to Netherby and leaning down close to his face.

The Gnomes were prepared for the Gnarlys to proclaim that Gnarly juju had saved North Woods from SsaA. The Gnomes were so sure that the Gnarlys were about to take credit for calling Nature back—and take no blame for chasing it away—their faces turned crimson red. Whittlesticks twitched in their hands.

"Nature back," said Nodwart just as the whittlesticks were raised, just as the wood thrush song rose again through the air.

Gnomes and Gnarlys turned away from their squabbling and followed the notes of the song as they soared high above Sweet Fat Mama, then filtered down through the trees.

"Nature has more juju than Gnarlys," Newt whispered as the last note fell to earth. Gnomes and Gnarlys followed the song's descent as if it were something they could see. Then, all nodded in agreement.

Though they had heard the bird's song for all the years of their lives, though the Gnarlys had fooled the Gnomes by mimicking the song hundreds of times before, it never sounded quite as it did at that moment.

"No Gnarly can match it," said the Wisest Gnome.

"No Gnome can store it in their Just-in-Case holes," returned Netherby.

By the end of the day, the songs and chortles, *wheeps* and *urps*, razzes and *eeks* fell to a murmur, and North Woods sounded more like the woods of October, instead of the woods of spring. For the first time in a long time, Nature was not only back, but back on schedule.

Netherby gave a huge yawn. It had been a very long time since he had nestled under his thistledown for a good, undisturbed sleep; a very long time since there weren't Gnomes every which way he turned.

"Now you Gnomes can get back to counting centipede legs, or whatever it is you do," Netherby said with a flick of his wrist.

He and the other Gnarlys were anxious to leave the entire unpleasant episode of angry Gnomes and crows and silent forest far, far behind. They were looking forward to a long nap inside Sweet Fat Mama. A nap that could go on for weeks.

The Gnomes, for their part, had every reason to run the Gnarlys out of North Woods, but they had had quite enough of Gnarlys for one season. There was a lot of work to catch up on.

With a *harrumph* in the direction of the Gnarlys, the Gnomes hoisted *How Nature Works* between them, turned, and stomped off down Highbush Hill without another word.

The Gnarlys gave a sigh of relief that was so big it ruffled the tailcoat of the last departing Gnome.

They, too, had had quite enough of Gnomes.

∽◉∾

If you think that the Gnarlys learned their lesson, and that, thereafter, the Gnomes and Gnarlys lived together peacefully in North Woods, you would be wrong.

By winter of that same year, the Gnarlys had repeatedly raided the Gnomes' store of pollen cakes and honeycomb. A Gnarly expedition lured the Foolish Gnome into a gooble trap (which made his reputation as the Foolish Gnome stick even harder), and the drop nets, catapults, and pitch spills were back in place at the entrance of Sweet Fat Mama.

The feud, I guess, will continue for another century or so.

Did Newt get his juju back? That's another story, I'm afraid, and it's getting late.

But, please, come again.

Field Note

When you walk in the woods, don't just look up and around, but down as well. Look under mushrooms, into the crevices of stone walls, between grasses and fern and under leaves. Who knows what you may find there?

About the Author & Illustrator

⤳✺⤶

Mary Cuffe Perez, author of six books, lives in the upstate New York town of Galway with her husband, Ken. She is an amateur naturalist -- a "woods roamer" -- and much of her writing is inspired and informed by the fields and forests of upstate New York. In addition to children's novels, she has published poetry and creative non-fiction. Visit her website at www.marycuffeperez.com.

Sallie Way is a high school art teacher who lives on a small farm in Galway, NY, with her husband, Greg, and an assortment of animals. Her passion for horses, gardening, art and the outdoors takes her to many interesting and beautiful places in the Adirondacks and beyond.

www.ingramcontent.com/pod-product-compliance
Lightning Source LLC
Chambersburg PA
CBHW030129260626
47156CB00008B/2858